Escape From Devil's Den

The Walls Of Time Will Be Breached

Tony —
Here's Your Free Book (Again)

Joe D.

Hope you Like The Sequel

Joe DeSantis

First published by Dog Ear Publishing
4010 W. 86th Street, Ste H
Indianapolis, IN 46268
www.dogearpublishing.net

ISBN: 978-1-4575-2626-8

This book is printed on acid-free paper.
Printed in the United States of America

To the late Dr. Paul Cortissoz,
Chairman, Dept. of English, Manhattan College.

TABLE OF CONTENTS

CHAPTER 1

The Dust Settles

T here is enormous power hidden within the pungent stench of death. It immediately redirects one's attention, interrupts the normal breathing process, sparks ghastly images of decay, and generally frightens the bejesus out of anyone unfortunate enough to be caught downwind of it.

That was the setting the fates had ordained for the unfortunate residents of Gettysburg in early July of 1863. For three long days, Robert E. Lee's invading Army of Northern Virginia and George Meade's defending Army of the Potomac had battered each other in and around the Pennsylvania town with unimagined ferocity.

On July 4th, as the spent Rebels began their tortuous, snake-like retreat towards the safety of their beloved state of Virginia in a driving rain storm, close to 50,000 blue and gray clad soldiers lay dead, wounded, or missing, the bloody residue of a war brought on in no small part by bombastic Southern fire eaters and self-righteous New England abolitionists.

When the tantalizing whispers of a Confederate withdrawal proved to be true, scores of skittish residents quietly stepped out from their darkened, dirt floor basements, while others trickled slowly back into Gettysburg from the relative safety of nearby towns or outlying residences. Once their eyes beheld the pitiful, chopped up remnants of the two great armies, the enormous task of burying the dead and assisting the wounded became the common concern of all.

All but one that is—all but John Larson, erstwhile college student turned dreadful night creature, who had also become a powerful secret weapon in the arsenal of the Federal army. His one remaining thread of humanity, his "passion," was his love for the Union, and he had put his powers to good use, attacking and disabling five secessionist generals involved in the battle for Gettysburg, including the commanding general Robert E. Lee himself.

For nearly four days and nights after the Confederate retreat he had remained hidden atop the northern half of the beautiful red brick Evergreen Cemetery Gatehouse, lying inside a crawl space between the roof top and the second floor bedroom.

The building had been put to good use as a temporary hospital for Union casualties, thereby making any movement on his part problematic. He could easily have accessed the roof and taken to the sky, but the constant ebb and flow of military personnel in and around Cemetery Hill made detection a very real possibility.

So he waited patiently, for the pitiful moans and shrieks of the wounded to taper off, for the army doctors to cease barking instructions to frazzled orderlies, and for the kind of silence that only an empty dwelling can supply when its inhabitants have left. That is a silence that hangs heavy in the air, and when one enters such a place, the first thought is to tread lightly in an effort to keep the mood of the room unbroken, as though the room itself was keeping a glaring, watchful eye on an uninvited guest.

Unfortunately, when that golden silence finally arrived, so had the dawn; this made it impossible for John to move about as he had hoped. He was keenly aware of the need to feed in the not too distant future, but that could only be accomplished during the evening. He had just resigned himself to another 12 hours of inactivity when he heard the faint sound of footsteps and muffled voices.

Both increased in intensity until the front door slowly creaked open. Perhaps the ones about to enter were loath to discover the severity of destruction left behind. They were of course sublimely ignorant of what lay listening intently in the attic. Had they known, the reaction would either be stunned disbelief or abject terror.

"Goodness gracious, it is as we feared, father. The house is a shambles, and so many of our belongings are broken or missing" stated a woman with forced resignation. John immediately recognized the voice as belonging to Elizabeth Thorn, wife of Peter Thorn, the cemetery caretaker.

He knew her from the summers he worked as a clerk at Fahnestock Brothers store on Baltimore Street. She would come shopping for provisions occasionally with her two young boys in tow, a plain but pleasant looking woman with dark hair pulled back, and slim features. John always thought that she possessed an inner strength far and above that of most women.

She continued on. "I truly can't blame the poor wounded, or the surgeons for that matter. The situation was indeed dire, and the fighting was fierce. But those Rebel soldiers! Every blessed window in the gatehouse is broken. Now the flies have infested all of the rooms, and that horrible stench! We will be unable to keep it out. I fear for the health of the children."

An older man answered. "And don't forget YOURSELF. You must remember not to tax your body too severely. As to the stench, there's a score of rotting horses in front of the house, and more lying over yonder in the field. We can be thankful that they are animals, my dear, and not people.

At least a fair number of the combatants have been temporarily buried, although placing some near our water pump

3

was certainly accomplished with little foresight to the future. We must now do what we can to make this place livable once again."

"I fear we will have scarce little time for that, father. Mr. McConaughy has already instructed me to stake out and prepare graves in the cemetery for our dead soldiers as fast as we possibly can. There is no time to waste."

"And how are we to accomplish THAT?" replied the old man with a hint of bitterness. "Peter has been gone for almost a year now with his regiment. We can be expected to muddle through with normal caretaking duties as best we can, what with my age and your delicate condition.

But no one could have imagined such a catastrophe right here in our midst. I don't see HIM volunteering to come and lend a hand with the graves, the pompous bastard."

"Now father, we will do what we must, as will everyone. The entire town is in a sorry state of affairs. Mother can watch the children and clean up inside while we work outdoors, and I will get word to some friends to lend a hand if they can.

But first let us see to the broken pump. Hopefully, it just needs minor repairs and a re-priming. We should all tent in the back yard until the house is cleansed."

John smirked briefly. If Mrs. Thorn had an inkling that a night creature was using her own attic as a base of operations, she would have been thinking more about those damned Freemasons than soap and water, he thought wryly to himself. They had him very nearly trapped in a warehouse off of Railroad Street about a week ago.

Only speed, strength, and sheer luck prevented his destruction at the hands of the forsworn enemy of his kind, resulting in their own unexpected rendezvous with the hereafter, wherever that may be. But one of the ambushers had managed to break free, and despite John's fervent offer to continue targeting rebel officers only, no bargain could be struck. That meant the loss of his most powerful weapon of all—anonymity.

Freemasons on both sides would now put aside their differences in this "civil war" and band together as a society of brothers to relentlessly hunt down and kill him at any cost. It had been their way around the world for so many hundreds of years, John mused, that even the possible dissolution of the United States could not change their singular focus.

And so he waited patiently in the attic crawl space as morning passed into afternoon, and then into dusk; Elizabeth and her family finally settled down in their tent to what would become many fitful nights of sleep. The rotting stench from the dead horses, coupled with the incessant annoyance from the hordes of black flies, would try their patience and fortitude, not to mention their overall health.

John sensed that evening had arrived. He crawled effortlessly on his back to the trap door that led onto the gatehouse rooftop, and then swung it quietly up and over. A quarter-moon stared down inquisitively as he slowly pulled himself up through the opening and onto the roof. There was a slight breeze that seemed to push the stark odor of decay onto the landscape, not that it mattered to him.

John stood up and beheld a beautiful overview of the town. From his perched vantage point, Gettysburg survived its three day ordeal relatively unscathed, at least in a structural sense. The rebels appeared to have taken care not to target any buildings with their artillery. For that John grudgingly gave them credit.

It may have been the result of an inbred sense of southern chivalry; he did not know. This General Lee of theirs was a true gentleman, even in the midst of battle. However, nothing would stop John in his mission to thwart their efforts to divide the nation, not even the veiled threat of retaliation from the Vampire Council, whatever that was.

While the town was generally spared the tremendous destructive power of shot and shell, Evergreen Cemetery, on the other hand, did receive a share of bumps and bruises, as it was well within the Union's defensive line. John glanced back over his shoulder and slowly scanned the immediate vicinity. It was not a particularly pretty sight.

There were splintered trees, ravaged shrubs, twisted iron fencing, an occasional dead animal, a handful of damaged monuments, and surprisingly, numerous headstones lying flat on the ground; and yet they were undamaged.

He found that to be a particularly strange sight in light of the fierce martial activity. The Union soldiers positioned in and around the cemetery during the enemy artillery barrage must have found their location both surreal and terrifying.

As they hugged the ground for whatever sliver of safety they could find, just a few feet below them lay what they were trying desperately not to become. When John vaulted from the roof and glided effortlessly to the ground, his eyes fixed upon a delicious slice of black humor.

It was a small, battered wooden sign. He looked about to make certain that the Thorns were settled in their tent for the night. There was a candle burning within, silhouetting Elizabeth as she tended to her children in their make-shift beds. A good woman to be sure, John thought as he stepped carefully over to the unintended novelty.

He picked it up off the ground, brushed off the dirt, and read the one sentence message quietly to himself. It read simply:

All Persons Found Using Firearms In These Grounds Will Be Prosecuted With The Utmost Rigor Of The Law

"How completely and utterly bizarre," he muttered as he shook his head in disbelief. "A hundred years from now, no one will ever believe that such a supreme bit of irony the likes of this ever existed." That said, he snapped the sign in half against his upraised knee and tossed it into a nearby shell hole.

It was then that John heard the faint sound of footsteps. Someone was moving quickly towards him. If that person happened to be Elizabeth, he had a much bigger problem than just worrying about the Freemasons.

She would recognize him at once, and for all intents and purposes, John Larson had been declared legally dead for almost two years now, courtesy of a deliciously devious scheme hatched in Louisiana by John and his master, Jacques Dumaine.

Why John's thoughts ventured back to Etenel Babako, the Louisiana plantation where his old life ended and his new one began, he did not know. He'd been having recurring premonitions that something had gone terribly wrong down along the Mississippi's River Road. The connection with Dumaine was broken, although he was unaware that he had even possessed this bond until it was summarily severed.

However, John had bigger fish to fry at the moment. He stood still with his back turned, waiting to be addressed by the approaching stranger. If it was indeed Elizabeth, all he could think of at that moment was to would blurt out that he was checking on a loved one's grave and simply walk off in the opposite direction without so much as a by your leave. But that contingency proved to be unnecessary, as the voice he heard directed at him was that of a man, with the same deep tonal quality as from earlier in the day.

"Pardon me. Evergreen is closed during the evening hours. Is there perhaps something that I can help you with?"

John turned and faced the man who he believed to be Elizabeth Thorn's father. "Ah, no sir, but thank you anyway. I was merely curious and wished to check for myself on any battle damage to the cemetery. It is well known as a beautiful place for solitude and reflection."

"Yes, it certainly is," he agreed with caution, "although it would have served you better had you come in the daytime. But I don't believe that I have had the pleasure. My name is John Masser. My daughter and I are tending to the cemetery at the moment. At least we are trying our best. And you are…?"

John's eyes danced about quickly for a lifeline, and found one. He looked over the man's shoulder and his gaze rested on the Baltimore Pike just beyond the gatehouse entrance. "My name is John also….John Pike." The man quickly eyed him up and down with suspicion.

"Do you…reside here in Gettysburg, Mr. Pike?"

"No, I am originally from York, and have been travelling of late. I heard news of the battle and thought that I would see for myself and also check on the condition of some old friends in town, the Garlachs. Are you acquainted with them?"

John hoped that Masser did not, and he was relieved with the reply. "I have heard the name spoken now and again by my daughter, but we have not actually met."

That did the trick, and the man dropped his guard. "See here, I am sorry about the questions, young man, but we have experienced problems on the battlefield over the past few days."

John's interest was piqued. "What kind of problems?"

Masser sighed dejectedly. "As if slaughtering each other on a grand scale over an issue such as slavery is not bad enough, now we have people, ghouls I call them, wandering the battle-field stripping the dead of their personal items. It is the final indignity."

He went on. "Of course, there are those who are of a different opinion. Why waste valuables by burying them with the dead, they say. My reply is that those miscreants are only trying justifying their own disgraceful behavior."

John was surprised at this revelation. "And what happens to them if they are caught in the act?"

"If they are Union soldiers, very little, I am sorry to say. But should they be civilians found picking the pockets of the dead or scavenging the battlefield to sell military items, then jail or even burial detail may be in their future; and believe me, burial detail right now is something to be avoided at all cost."

He paused for a moment. "I am sorry, Mr. Pike. It would appear that I need to step off of my pulpit. Caring for the dead in a proper, respectful way is very important to our family, and I fear we will have much work to do in the immediate future.

Anyway, I believe that I am a fair judge of character, and I can tell that you are a young man who values human decency and Christian ideals. What would you say to that assessment?"

John barely contained a laugh that exploded deep from within. He closed his eyes, nodded and humbly replied "Amen, brother!"

CHAPTER 2

The Scent of Carnage

John looked briefly back over his shoulder while waving as he walked along the Baltimore Pike, then raised his voice. "Goodbye, Mr. Masser. I will try to help you with the burials later on in the week." He turned and muttered quietly to himself "Much later."

"Thank you Mr. Pike. I fear we will need all the help we can get." The voice from the darkness surrounding the cemetery gatehouse sounded hopeful but cautious. "Remember the great task ahead of us, for the soldiers' sake.

They deserve a proper burial for their sacrifice. It is the least that we can do for them and their loved ones." A nice young man, Masser concluded; a bit on the cold side, but a proper gentleman.

Additional smells now wafted over John as he made his way slowly towards his anticipated destination, the diamond shaped green belt near the center of town, smells that were of a much more familiar nature.

Besides the overpowering reek of decaying, putrid flesh, the scent of urine and feces blended in quite effortlessly to reach a magnificent and robust olfactory crescendo. The devil himself could not have concocted a more noxious mixture in the ninth circle of hell.

Of course, it did not bother John in the slightest, and the more he thought about the situation, that is, thousands of soldiers draining their innards throughout every street, backyard, and garden in Gettysburg for three days would certainly have given the townsfolk the image of living within an immense outhouse. A closer inspection of the landscape showed hordes of buzzing flies gorging themselves on intermittently spaced, crusty brown mounds.

That must have made for a nice change of pace for them besides feasting on the dead horses, mules, or men. And the strong ammonia smell from the fountains of urine spritzed about by man and beast was a constant reminder to all left behind that another problem existed even though it might not necessarily be seen.

"Seen" John whispered suddenly as he snapped himself out of his reverie. He really needed to pull himself together. He was officially a dead man, so being recognized during an evening stroll about town would make for quite the paradoxical situation.

He grabbed a Rebel's discarded slouch hat stuck on a nearby shrub and pulled it low over his forehead. Any kind of extended eye contact with passersby was also something that begged avoidance.

However, what could not be avoided for much longer was his insatiable need to feed. He felt weak and ravenous; a combination that would not bode well for anyone within his general proximity should the rule of targeting only the castoffs and scum of society be thrown to the wind. Blood was needed, and needed tonight.

John stopped by the Wagon Hotel on the cusp of the Emmitsburg Road. Federal sharpshooters had made good use of the three story building during the battle, and it showed the

11

pock marks of return fire from their angry Rebels counterparts looking for revenge.

The hotel was perfectly situated within the Union lines to be of immense help in keeping the Johnnies from getting too "comfortable" at their stations scattered throughout the town's windows, garrets, and barricades.

As John was inspecting the damage to the hotel, he heard the uneven tramping of feet coming from the direction of Brickyard Lane. A dozen or so dispirited Confederates passed by, heads down, filthy, with sullen faces. Some of them had gotten lost when separated from their retreating units, while others decided that they had seen enough of the war's slaughter and surrendered out of sheer mental or physical exhaustion.

Then there were those who had deserted with the intention of sneaking back to their farms and family in the South, as slim a chance as that was. The looming specter of incarceration in a prisoner of war camp was now in the immediate future for them all, and by the end of this conflict, there would be a fair chance that they would die in captivity of disease, starvation, abuse, or flat out neglect.

Unfortunately, that was an inconvenient truth whispered only in higher circles. The South had its share of hell holes, but its infrastructure was badly frayed, and Rebel prison guards fared little better than their Federal prisoners. The North, with all its abundance, simply withheld the basic necessities out of spite and revenge.

A young, nervous Union private was at the head of the rag tags, leading the way. He could not have been more than 17, and felt pity for the captured men; after all, they were just doing their duty like he was. An older soldier, a corporal, was off to the side, occasionally smiling whenever he prodded one with a rusty looking bayonet fixed to his Springfield. He was having a grand old time.

At the end of the parade was a fat, preening Federal officer riding on a tired looking brown gelding. He sat erect in the saddle with his right arm akimbo, and appeared to be quite proud of his catch, as though no one else could possibly have accomplished the daring feat of capturing lost, worn out, frightened men.

John was repelled by his air of self- importance. He was also under the false impression that a man could not possibly strut while on horseback. In this case, at least, he was terribly wrong.

"Prisoners move along," the officer bellowed for the benefit of no one but himself. "We will find a cozy spot for you soon enough; then you will wish you had never decided to visit Pennsylvania without an official invitation from Governor Curtin. Corporal, you're sure that none of these men are wounded?"

"Positive, lieutenant, at least not as yet" was the reply as he poked an unfortunate Rebel sharply in the butt, drawing blood.

This resulted in a howl of pain, followed by a vague statement from one of the other prisoners concerning the legitimacy of the corporal's birth. Everyone laughed except for one Rebel toward the back of the group. He was too busy focusing on John, so much so that he tripped over a piece of broken caisson wheel and fell to the ground.

John didn't notice him until his pratfall, but when the man got up and dusted himself off, he took a closer look at the soldier's features and immediately recalled their meeting; it was at Cashtown about a week ago, just before the start of the battle. This was the same Masonic orderly he had tricked at a hotel on the Chambersburg Pike for the expressed purpose of gaining entry to disable Confederate General A.P. Hill.

While the impromptu plan worked to perfection despite the dangers, was the orderly smart enough to put two and two together and realize that he had let in a night creature? The more important question begged, why wasn't the startled John alerted to his mortal enemy's presence?

Then it hit him; the smell of rotting meat had always been the principal way for his kind to detect Freemasons, but that luxury was now eliminated, thanks to the myriad of disgusting aromas fouling the air for miles around. The luxury of an advanced warning had been effectively eliminated. John had to rely solely on his wits and keen eyesight if he was to survive.

He knew that he needed to get away as soon as possible, and was mulling over this latest setback when a voice boomed its way toward him. "You there, in the slouch hat…stand fast." It was that pompous Federal officer. He reined his horse in John's direction while the ragamuffin parade came to a slow stop. "What is your business in Gettysburg? Be quick about it, boy."

John was in no mood for this fool; his anger was rising. The man was drawing attention to him, and that was the one thing to be avoided. He tried to keep the officer's horse as a sight buffer between him and the group that included that damned Freemason while he replied.

John replied innocently. "What seems to be the problem, general?" The guards tried unsuccessfully to stifle their laughter; that amusement indicated there was no love lost on their superior. The officer appeared to be visibly stung by the deliberate miscue, and John was pleased. He attempted to reply coolly to the verbal jab.

"I am a lieutenant, thank you," glancing menacingly toward his men. "I say again, what is your business here? Provost guards are rounding up all Rebels left behind in the retreat. How do I know that you are not one of them?

Many of the secessionists do not wear regular army uniforms, and go to battle in their civilian clothing. The town and surrounding area is infested with the vermin. Now, answer my question, and be quick about it."

John replied in a distinctly monotone voice, the only other way he could display his defiance...at the moment. He relished the thought of showing the lieutenant his full displeasure in the not too distant future. Much of what he said in his reply contained various elements of truth, the easier to remember should he have need of retelling it somewhere else down the line.

"My name is John Pike. I am originally from York, and am a student at the Agricultural College of Pennsylvania. I have just come from Evergreen Cemetery to see how the Thorn household has fared, and now I am off to check on some family friends, the Garlachs, who live on Baltimore Street. Henry, that is, Mr. Garlach, is a carpenter by trade, and a very good one, I daresay."

The lieutenant appeared to be genuinely disappointed with the answer to his question, but that did not stop him from abusing his power. It mattered little what John actually said. He had a score to settle with this upstart, and he was not about to ignore an affront to his dignity.

"Just the same, I think we will take you in for some questioning. Now get in line with the rest of this rabble and be quick about it."

John decided that he had endured enough. He walked slowly toward his tormentor, and as he grew nearer, the officer's horse reared slightly, its wide eyes with a fear that went unnoticed.

John reached out and placed a hand over the lieutenant's ankle. The man gasped and jerked as a stabbing jolt of terror ran up his leg and permeated his entire body. John stared at him with controlled malice; his voice was low and steady.

"You will do nothing of the kind. I will go about my business, and you will do the same." His grip on the ankle tightened. He knew that if he applied just a bit more pressure, the bone would snap like a dry twig. That would be enjoyable, but counter-productive to his purpose.

The lieutenant blinked several times in rapid succession and attempted to speak, but could only manage a raspy squeak. He cleared his throat while backing the grateful horse away. His face was one of bewilderment mixed with genuine horror.

"Go…go on about your business….whatever…it…is. All right you prisoners; get back into line. We're leaving right now. Move them out, private."

The captives resumed their solemn march into town, but the orderly John had tried so hard to avoid contact with had by now put the pieces of the puzzle together. He continued the trek with renewed vigor; his face had a look of determination and purpose seldom seen on a prisoner of war. The good fortune John experienced during the three day battle at Gettysburg had all the appearances of petering out.

He continued on his way along Baltimore Street. Many of the town's residents were up and about despite the evening hour, and it did not take long to discover why. A small group of men were gathered in front of the Rupp House. John passed by them slowly to catch a bit of their conversation.

"This stench is absolutely horrific. We have been left with an intolerable situation here, gentlemen. I for one don't know how much longer I can stand it." The man looked to be at his wits end.

Another piped in after taking in a deep breath from a handkerchief balled up in his fist. John detected the scent of lilac. "I understand your feelings completely, Mr. Sweney, but now that relief efforts from out of town have increased, it is only a matter of time before we should begin to see marked improvement."

The last man began to speak, but suddenly gagged several times, causing the others in the group to casually take three steps backwards, as though the surreal dance was now a common practice in Gettysburg. He vomited his dinner smack in the middle of their circle.

"Sorry my friends," he said with a mixture of embarrassment and disgust while wiping his mouth on a sleeve. "I made a poor decision an hour ago. I said to myself, McCreary, go ahead and have that second slice of peach pie for dessert." He paused and glanced down.

"This is the result. Well, it's off to bed, although I for one continue to have the devil of a time trying to sleep with all of the windows shut tight. Pick your poison, I say; this stench or the July heat. Either one will keep you up half the night." The others shook their heads in agreement, and offered their good-nights with a nod or a wave.

A very interesting conversation, John thought to himself. So outside agencies have come to the aid of Gettysburg. The clash must have taken a severe toll on both armies; just how severe remained to be seen. More information was needed, but there were just too many uncomfortable townspeople still milling about to insure that his inquiries were to be completely safe.

John had no desire to tempt fate and be recognized, so a change in route was necessary. As he prepared to abandon the more heavily trafficked Baltimore Street, a cart drawn by an ancient looking mule ambled to a stop. A sad faced driver hopped off and made his way to the back, grabbing a shovel off a side rack as he went.

He tugged at a bandana tied around his neck and pulled it up and over his mouth and nose, giving him a roguish, high-wayman-like appearance. All that was missing was a sword and pistol to be brandished from each hand. But there would be no daring robberies of fine ladies baubles this night.

He scooped a shovelful of white powder from a pile on the cart bed and flung it across his body into a large rut in the road. It had filled up with some sort of foul smelling muck that had become a popular meeting place for black flies.

John stopped and watched with interest. The man made a grunt of pleasure as the flies scattered from their unwelcome shower. Many of them flew a few feet in the air, dropped to the ground, twitched for a few moments, and then lay still.

"Die slow, you little bastards, and good riddance," he said smiling with great satisfaction. The wind changed towards John, giving him the answer to his unspoken question—the powder was chloride of lime, a substance composed of calcium hydroxide, chloride, and hypochlorite. It was used either as a bleaching agent or a disinfectant.

Now it was John's turn to smile, albeit ruefully. That definition jumped out of his thoughts with gusto as a result of his time enrolled at the Agricultural College of Pennsylvania. It also cast his mind back again to Louisiana and Etenel Babako, the plantation where he had been transformed into a night creature, or vampire, as the fools and the misinformed were so quick to spout.

He hated that word…"vampire." The hierarchy of the Freemasons and Catholic Church had full knowledge that he and his kind targeted for slaughter only the wicked and the outcasts of society, yet both organizations relentlessly pursued and decimated their ranks throughout the civilized world with righteous indignation. It appeared that nothing could be said or done to alter their singular focus.

But was it not Christian teaching that God was the Supreme Being who made ALL things, and if that were true, how could God create something evil? John was snapped out of his reverie by the muffled voice of the cart driver.

"Hey there, young fella; you lookin' fur work? The smell is what it is, but the pay ain't half bad, and you'll be doin' a great service, specially for the women folk n' children."

He hung the shovel over his shoulder and ambled over with guarded anticipation. "So…whatcha say? I been given the power to hires anyone I damn please that can stomach the job.

Are you up to it? Lordy, I could surely use some help. There ain't but half a dozen of us right now spreadin' this stuff all around the town to cover over the blood and such." He finished his plea with a loud wheeze, followed by a series of coughs.

John was genuinely amused. "That's a very tempting offer, my friend, but I am afraid that I must decline your offer, as I have personal business to attend to. By the way, you should take greater care not to breathe in the lime. It attacks the alveoli in the lungs, and once that occurs, the damage is often irreversible, I am afraid.

You would do well to wash your eyes out with some clean water also. I can see that they're awfully bloodshot, and can become infected if not attended to in a timely fashion."

The man cocked his head and stared at John as though he had two heads. "I can't tell if you're pullin' my leg or if you're just one smartass son of a bitch... but I'll keep it in mind just the same. What I'd really like to know is what you're usin' to keep these goddamned flies away. I don't see a blessed one lightin' on you, boy; that ain't natural."

"Mister, believe me when I say that natural's got NOTHING to do with it."

CHAPTER 3

Interesting Changes

John briefly continued his walk on Baltimore Street before turning right at High Street, and then left onto Stratton Street. Pedestrian traffic had decreased as he had hoped, and it would not be long before he would be at his chosen destination, the grassy diamond near the middle of town. Loose talk and information would be at a premium there.

As he passed Middle Street, he glanced on the ground and noticed a tattered, crumpled newspaper. He picked it up and scanned the masthead. It was a copy of The New York Times dated July 8th. How in blazes had this ended up in Gettysburg?

Then he remembered the conversation of the three men. Outside agencies had arrived to help the town and the wounded. It would come as no surprise that people would bring newspapers from different locales. This could prove to be a very useful find.

John flattened the paper against his chest, and then turned it to the front page. He immediately found what he was looking for. A headline read: **"Great Jubilation—Speeches by the President, Secretary Stanton, General Halleck, and Others."** A quick scan ended up a quarter way down the column—*8PM: A crowd assembled in front of the National Hotel, and marched up*

Pennsylvania Avenue, headed by the Marine Band, to the Executive Mansion, serenaded and enthusiastically cheered the President, with repeated cheers for Generals Grant, Meade, Rosecrans, the Armies of the Union, etc. The President appeared at the window, amid loud cheers and said:

"Fellow citizens, I am very glad indeed to see you all tonight, and yet I will not say I thank you for this call but I do most sincerely thank Almighty God for the occasion on which you have called. How long ago is it? Eighty odd years since on the 4th of July for the first time in the history of the world a nation, by its representatives, assembled and declared as a self-evident truth, that all men are created equal.

That was the birthday of the United States of America. Since then the 4th of July has had several very peculiar recognitions. The two most distinguished men in the framing and the support of the Declaration were Thomas Jefferson and John Adams—the one having penned it, and the other sustained it the most forcibly in debate—the only two of the fifty-five who sustained it being elected President of the United States.

Precisely fifty years after they put their hands to the paper, it pleased Almighty God to take both from this stage of action. This was indeed an extraordinary and remarkable event in our history. Another President, five years after, was called from this stage of existence on the same day and month of the year; and now in this last 4th of July, just passed.

When we have a gigantic rebellion at the bottom of which is an effort to overthrow the principle that all men were created equal, we have the surrender of a most powerful position and army on that very day, and not only so, but in a succession of battles in Pennsylvania, near to us. Through three days, so rapidly fought that they might be called one great battle on the 1st, 2nd, and 3rd of the month of July; and on the 4th the cohorts of those who opposed the Declaration that all men are created equal, turned and ran.

Gentlemen, this is a glorious theme, and the occasion for a speech, prepared to make one worthy of the occasion. I would like to speak in terms of praise due to the many brave offices and soldiers who have fought in the cause of the Union and liberties of their country from the beginning of the war. These are trying occasions, not only in success, but for the want of success.

I dislike mentioning the name of one single officer, lest I might do wrong to those I might forget. Recent events bring up glorious names, and particularly prominent ones, but these I will not mention. Having said this much, I will now take the music."

John was a bit bewildered by the text of the speech, so he re-read it a second time to take in the ramifications. Mr. Lincoln appeared to be pressing home the point of human equality more than the unbreakable covenant that was the United States.

The Rebels had been repulsed at Gettysburg; a victory for the secessionists would have given Lee a number of choice military options, any of which could very well have brought about the end of the war, and the dissolution of the Union.

Yet, rather than ram home the point of ensuring the country's unity, Lincoln spoke first and foremost about equality. Of course, that meant freeing the slaves. Somehow, between the times that John left college to his attacks on the high command in the Army of Northern Virginia, war aims had expanded. Or perhaps this was another vital war aim that Mr. Lincoln had harbored all along.

He read on intently: *At the close of the President's speech the crowd proceeded to the War Department, and serenaded and cheered Mr. Stanton. The Secretary appeared on the steps, and made a short, stirring speech. He said that something under two years ago, on receipt of an offer of conditional surrender from a Rebel Army, the General in command replied: "I propose to move immediately on your works." The same General again moved on the enemy's works, and the result is Vicksburg."*

He paid many flattering compliments to General Grant, also to General Meade. He concluded by saying "The same strategy, the same bravery, the same indomitable zeal, which have driven the enemy from the banks of the Mississippi, and the banks of the Susquehanna, will, in a very short period, drive every armed rebel from the field, and every Copperhead to his den."

The Secretary next introduced Major General Halleck, who was received with applause. He alluded to the time when he first took command of the Western Army, two years ago. Since then Grant has been under his command. He had fought 15 battles and won 15 victories. He was in Vicksburg on the 4th, and he will be in Port Hudson tomorrow or the next day.

This was fantastic news! The same time that Meade sent Lee packing for an early return trip down South, General Grant had captured the vitally important fortress city of Vicksburg. John immediately conjured up the image of a map of the United States in his head.

This victory meant that the Mississippi River was now under Federal control, effectively splitting the Confederacy in two, and enabling transports to easily ferry Union troops to designated points deep within the South, virtually at will.

And what else was it that was said about Grant—15 battles and 15 victories? Could it be possible? The Western Theater of Operations appeared to be secure; perhaps it was time for the President to think about moving Grant closer to the action in the east.

Although General Meade had indeed won a great victory, it was strictly a defensive one; the Army of Northern Virginia was far from finished. The North needed a general who would be unafraid to confront Lee's fighting spirit head on.

But John was not so impressed with this General Halleck fellow, whoever he was. It seemed in his speech as though he was trying to grab some of Grant's thunder on the flimsy pretext of being his superior officer. As he continued on Stratton Street,

John wondered if Henry Halleck would be equally as willing to take some of the blame for any of Grant's failures.

Stumbling upon a copy of the New York Times was more than anything John could have possibly hoped for in the way of national information. Up to now he had to be content with collecting bits and pieces of news wherever he might be.

While it was a newspaper with a decidedly Yankee slant, there could be no denying that the two great triumphs of Gettysburg and Vicksburg were tilting the scales of victory in the direction of the United States, and not a moment too soon.

He finally reached York Street and veered left towards the diamond. As he grew closer he observed a commotion in front of a place he knew well, the Globe Inn. Everyone in Gettysburg was aware of its history. Originally built and owned by the town's founder, John Gettys, the building eventually became a principal meeting place for Democrat politicians and their supporters, of which there were many in the area.

The property was presently owned by Charles Will, a decent, hard-working gentleman whom John had met on numerous occasions while he boarded for two summers with the Garlachs on Baltimore Street. Mr. Will often spent time in Fahnestocks, John's place of employment. While picking out various items for the inn, Mr. Will would often talk to anyone who would listen about one of his favorite subjects, politics, while John filled his order from behind the counter.

Mr. Will was talking once again, but this time, he was up on the second floor balcony of the inn, pumping a closed fist at a crowd of angry men below; some were yelling back up at Mr. Will, calling him a filthy Democrat and a Copperhead, among other choice adjectives.

John was quite sure by the intensity of the hatred spewing that this was not going to end well. Since he would have been recognized, there was no way to come to the man's aid even if he wanted to. All he could do was stand back in the shadows and watch this passion play proceed towards its inevitable climax. He didn't have long to wait.

A small detachment of the army's provost guard marched up methodically from Carlyle Street and halted in front of the inn. A weary captain of the guard sighed and spoke calmly with the leader of the group, whose agitation had increased in intensity upon the arrival of what many residents now viewed as the law and power in town, at least until things reverted back to a semblance of normalcy. He stabbed a finger again and again up at the balcony while pressing his case at the top of his lungs.

"Captain, I am telling you that man is a Confederate sympathizer who gladly gave aid and comfort to the enemy at the same time that this town was being ransacked and our brave troops cut to ribbons. I want him arrested right now, do you hear? It is your sworn duty to..."

"Don't presume to tell me what my duty is" snarled the captain as he leaned forward, nearly nose to nose with the man, who suddenly snapped out of his frothy tirade with a quick flutter of eye blinks.

"I...I only...my apologies, sir. I did not mean to presume..."

He glanced about quickly to the others in his group, looking for support. "We believe that Charles Will is a traitor, and the loyal citizens of Gettysburg are prepared to offer proof of this claim. For three days he warmly welcomed Rebel officers to his inn, where they lived high on the hog while many of the residents were forced to cower in basements for fear of their lives.

We demand...I mean rather, request, that he be detained by the proper authorities until such time that charges can be formally presented and proved...yes, proved I say."

The captain appeared only vaguely satisfied, but he knew full well that he was in a difficult position. He turned to the balcony with one hand resting comfortably on the hilt of his sword and looked up. He was about to speak but was cut off before he could even open his mouth by Mr. Will, who had been listening intently all the while.

"That is a bold faced lie, sir; a lie fabricated by the damned Union League of Gettysburg. Those before you all members, aaaand they all are Republicans. This is nothing more than a vicious attempt to strike out at any and all Democrats in the town. The accusations are based solely on political bias, nothing more, and I will not surrender myself to anyone until…hold on, here he is now."

A fairly well dressed gentleman walked briskly up the street and stopped in front of the inn, waving an acknowledgement to the beleaguered Mr. Will. There was something about this man that John did not like.

He couldn't quite put his finger on it, but it was a mild case of revulsion mixed with anger, a feeling that he had experienced before. All it took was the opening sentence from the mystery man for John to remember what it was.

"Just a minute, captain. I am J. Casset Neely, lawyer and Mr. Wills' legal representative," he recited with a definite, puffed up air of superiority. "I must strongly protest the lynch mob atmosphere that has been allowed to proliferate at the very doorstep of my client, a pillar of the community and well-respected businessman. I trust that a man of your standing and intelligence is not entertaining any thoughts to arresting this innocent man?"

"There is no entertainment in my position, thank you" replied the captain brusquely. "I am here on a complaint to arrest Charles Will on suspicion of offering aid and comfort to the enemy. For the present, you may accompany him as his legal representative, but that is all. This is not the time or the place to wrangle over a man's guilt or innocence." He looked up to the balcony. "Mr. Will, you must come down directly or I will be obliged to send in my men."

Of course, a jurist! Now John understood. That was the reason for his quick animosity. How he despised the way they would routinely twist and subvert the rules of law to suit their clients' selfish, personal needs. They were a plague on society, and he recalled dispatching several of them in the past with great satisfaction. Perhaps it was time to rekindle that satisfaction, under the right set of circumstances. Besides, he still had not eaten.

A look of restrained anger came over Mr. Will; he nodded to the captain and his lawyer, then disappeared from view, but shortly thereafter walked out the front door and stepped in between the guards without a word.

"And what about his son, John" the leader of the mob asked with unabashed satisfaction. "John Will is just as guilty as his father. He gladly served the Rebels at the inn."

"All right then," the captain replied with a hint of distrust as he readied to leave. "Sergeant, locate John Will and bring him along. In the meantime, the rest of go back to your homes. I will take charge from here on in."

John watched as both soldiers and citizens departed in opposite directions. Fortunately, for the self-important Mr. Neely, he chose to follow up on the captain's offer and accompany his client under guard; otherwise, the night creature would have been more than happy to shred the lawyer's throat while feeling the man squirm helplessly in his grip. "What a pity," John whispered. "That would have been quite the satisfying kill."

From the distasteful scene that he had just witnessed, John came to the inescapable conclusion that any cooperation between Democrats and Republicans in the town, cooperation that had been forged during their recent ordeal, had quickly disintegrated.

The search for scapegoats was added to the business of returning Gettysburg to a semblance of normalcy. He thought it would be a wise policy for any Democrats in the immediate vicinity to keep a low profile, at least for the time being.

John had indeed obtained a bounty of information on this, his first night's walk after the battle, but his hunger had increased to the point that it could no longer be ignored. He needed to feed, and soon. As he reached the center of town, a strong scent of blood rose above all others. There was a food source nearby, and he had to find it.

Discovery was not the problem that he had supposed it would be. He simply followed his nose across the town square until he was on Chambersburg Street. John shortly zeroed in his destination, and he would be forced to summon all of his remaining strength if he were to obtain the sustenance he craved.

He stopped about half way down the block and stared across the road at a building that made him feel unclean, just like the first time he saw it—Christ Lutheran Church.

He had stood on the same spot at the curb more than a week ago, fantasizing over the blood of a murdered priest that was dripping down the front steps. The chaplain had been shot dead for refusing to hand over his sword to a passing Confederate who was in no mood for the proprieties of war.

The beautiful, cupola topped church, replete with ornate white columns, had been used extensively as an emergency hospital for wounded Union soldiers, and judging from the smells and sounds coming out of it, nothing had changed. John sneered; despair, pain, and death were the new communicants at the shining altar of the all merciful God.

The building reeked of blood and gore right down through to the basement, but there was no possible way for John to enter. Then again, perhaps he did not have to. He noticed an odd looking mound towards the rear of the building and decided to investigate.

It was a pile of amputated arms and legs, covered by hundreds of flies, larvae, and other crawling insects, grim souvenirs of the butchery that had gone on and was still going on inside the house of the Lord.

This certainly was not the bountiful feast that John had envisioned, but it would have to do on short notice. He went down on his knees and unceremoniously began scattering the limbs about, searching for the fresh ones he assumed would be on top. He was not wrong in his assumption.

A still warm leg cut off right up to the thigh bone held an ample supply of blood. He lifted it above his head and drank deeply, his mouth turning scarlet as he furiously sucked the limb dry to extract every precious drop. As he tossed it away, flies followed in hot pursuit and quickly had it completely covered once again. It was no small wonder why the residents of Gettysburg hated them so.

John soon discovered that arms were not worth the trouble; they held very little blood, and the contortions of the hands made them visually unappetizing. Some were stiffly gnarled as though still suffering infinite pain, while others were outstretched in a veritable handshake position, belying their new status as useless pieces of discarded flesh.

Legs were definitely the limb of choice, and there were many to choose from, courtesy of the rifled musket and its constant companion, the bone shattering mini ball.

John was just putting the finishing touches to his dinner when a cold breeze brushed over him from behind, forcing him to shudder. This was quite a feat, considering the fact that it was July AND he was already stone dead.

He rose up and turned to face the street, only to catch a glimpse of a cloaked figure walking towards the diamond. He could not make out the face, and was about to shrug off the incident when he imagined he heard a fading voice utter the words "Bon appetite."

CHAPTER 4

The Past Comes To Light

A lone horseman cantered casually on the River Road, passing one beautiful plantation after another straddled alongside the winding Mississippi River. The temperature was unusually warm, even by Louisiana standards.

He removed his hat and wiped the sweat from his brow on his sleeve, which had long since reached a darker blue color than the rest of his uniform, then reached for a canteen and took a long, slow swig of lukewarm water. He spat most of it out in a tight stream onto the ground.

"That was less than refreshing, I can assure you, Suzy," he said to his horse in a casual, matter of fact tone. The horse pricked up her ears but made no other motion as she continued on her way. "We should reach our destination by high noon, if my calculations are correct; then you can get a cool rub down, a bag of feed, and some rest. I promise old girl."

He patted the horse affectionately, and continued on in silence. There was much to think about, but this was not the time to let thoughts trail off to mundane matters. He knew that his fact finding mission would be of great importance should the rumors and innuendos prove to be true and more than just superstitious slave talk.

Within the hour he halted before two long rows of massive oaks covered in Spanish moss, and peered down a green corridor to a red bricked mansion with gleaming white columns on its front. "Well, I suppose this is Etenel Babako. At least the descriptions of its beauty are true. One can only speculate about the rest. All right then, old girl, let's finish this journey."

No sooner had the words been spoken than another blue rider worked his way up the shaded path from the plantation, waving his hat in the air as he rode. "Hello there; Captain Fuerst, I presume? Lieutenant Shannon at your service; I've been keeping an eye out for you all morning."

He reached the end of the path and smartly saluted his superior officer, who returned the salute with a slight smile. "There is no further need for any more of that, lieutenant. We are all...**on the level**...are we not?"

The smile was returned, and the question answered. "We are. I too **am a widow's son.**"

The two men then reached out very deliberately, with each man extending his right hand. It started out as an ordinary handshake, but quickly morphed. The captain pressed the top of his thumb over the second knuckle of the lieutenant, who did likewise in return.

With the preliminaries out of the way, the fellow Freemasons spoke freely and to the point. "You have come directly from Baton Rouge, I take it?"

"Yes, a warm four hour ride, to be sure, but it was of the utmost importance that I get here as quickly as possible to investigate these...stories. How long have you been here, lieutenant?"

"Two days, sir."

"And you have interrogated...excuse me; that was a poor choice of words. You have spoken to the principals involved?"

The lieutenant shrugged. "It has been difficult to find out just who the principals are, I'm afraid. The slaves aren't saying much now, but I believe that they all shared terrifying experiences at one time or another here on this plantation. It's the perfect location, sir; isolated, self-sufficient, often forgotten, just the setting…for a vampire's lair."

"So you believe the stories, then" the captain said ominously. The lieutenant shook his head and paused.

"I'll reserve judgment on that until we've both had a chance to question the slaves from a list that I've put together. When would you like to start, sir?"

"There's no time like the present, Shannon. If you could get someone to tend to my horse, we can begin at a place of your choosing. I take it that those on your list are readily available?"

"Yes; they don't know where else to go, sir, to be honest. Many of them have spent their entire lives here, so knowledge of the outside world is hard to come by."

The two Union officers worked their way down the greenbelt pathway in silence until they came to the front of the mansion house. A young Negro boy of about 12 burst out of the entrance door and took hold of the horses' reins.

"I wuz waitin' too, suh. Willie will takes care o' dem now."

The men dismounted and the boy eagerly led their horses towards the barn. "Let us get protocol out of the way," Fuerst said matter of factly. "Introduce me to the owner and we can get this investigation started."

Shannon responded cautiously. I'm sorry, sir; the owner, a Mr. Jacques Dumaine, is nowhere to be found."

"An owner has actually left his plantation? I'll be damned. Well then, let us meet with the head overseer."

"That conversation would prove a bit one-sided, sir. You see, his grave is over yonder to the right, at least what's left of it. It's been…desecrated."

Fuerst raised an eyebrow. "He must have been a charming fellow; and what about the remaining overseers?"

"Ahhh…missing sir."

"Lieutenant, just who WAS in charge here when the local authorities got wind that something might be wrong and decided to pay a visit?"

"Actually, a paddle wheeler passed the plantation's dock one night and all the slaves were seen celebrating like it was Mardi Gras; a veritable hoop n' holler, I'm told, complete with torches, singing and dancing…you name it, sir."

"That IS interesting; so there were no white people on the ENTIRE plantation, and the preliminary information sent to me stated it is what, 1000 acres? No authority presence at ALL?"

The two men climbed the steps to the short porch of the mansion house. "So it would appear, sir. The investigation can begin right here and now if you wish. We will need to talk to several of the house slaves anyway. I will get them."

As the lieutenant went indoors, Fuerst sat down in a wicker rocking chair and took out a cigar. He never got the chance to strike a match. His assistant returned with a pregnant Negro woman, who looked to be about 20 years old. She waddled in slowly due to her delicate condition, holding a glass of mint water, which she presented to the captain.

He responded gratefully. "Thank you, my dear. This is greatly appreciated, I assure you. Please have a seat and get comfortable."

Shannon provided the necessary introductions. "Mary, this is Captain Fuerst. He's come from Baton Rouge to ask you a few questions, if you don't mind."

"And what if I do mind?" she responded fearfully.

"Mary, we are here to help, and would be grateful for any information that you could provide to us."

The girl relaxed and took a deep sigh. "All right, captain; what is it you want to know?"

"I understand that you are a house servant here at the plantation, and that you tended to the needs of Mr. Dumaine, the plantation's owner, is that not correct?"

"I am a slave sir, not a servant. The rest of what you said is true."

Fuerst responded with a pained look. "When the war is over, my dear, everyone will be free. That's what this war is about now."

He continued. "Did Mr. Dumaine treat you well?"

Mary tried to hide a sneer. "I was his slave, sir. He treated me any way he wanted to at the time."

"I see. Let me go further; did he seem...unusual in any way...have any peculiar habits, things of that nature?"

Mary shifted in her chair. "He only went round the house and grounds at night. Everyone was afraid of him, even the overseers; all except Algernon. You see, Mr. Dumaine was so strong, and when he looked at you"....her voice trailed off and her eyes grew wider.

The captain leaned forward. "Do you know where Mr. Dumaine is now, Mary?"

The girl seemed suddenly satisfied, like a pretty black cat that had just eaten a sparrow. She replied with a hint of a smile. "Who can say where white folks go?"

Shannon interrupted. "If you please, Mary; I have made an extensive search of the house and grounds in the time that I have been here. Other than the damaged grave of this Algernon fellow, the only other thing out of the ordinary was a burnt rocking chair on the second floor balcony of the master bedroom. Do you know anything about that?

She stared off into the distance and replied icily. "I don't know nothin' bout nothin', sir.

The lieutenant sighed. "All right, Mary... I believe that will be all. Would you kindly tell Annette that we would like to talk to her now?"

The young woman grabbed both side arms of the wicker chair and slowly rose to a standing position. "Yes, sir; I will fetch her directly."

The two men exchanged glances as they waited until she stepped inside the house. "Do you see what I'm talking about, captain? There has been definite resistance on the part of the slaves to reveal what they know. Mary, although more refined than most, is a perfect example of...."

He stopped speaking as a middle aged woman stepped out onto the porch while wringing her hands. She was the opposite of Mary in many ways—worn out, scowling, and quite unattractive. But there was one thing they both had in common, and that was a look of fear.

"Annette, I am Captain Glessner. I'd like to ask you a few questions. Won't you sit down?"

The response was nearly combative. "I prefer to stand, sir, if you don't mind."

"Fine; I understand that you have been here for quite some time, is that not so?"

"I've lived here all my life; that's quite some time...sir."

"Yes, well, can you enlighten us as to the whereabouts of Mr. Dumaine and the overseers employed here on the plantation? I understand there were six of them, not counting the head over-seer.

"I don't know nothin' bout them, sir. Iz a house slave, and don't worry bouts what goes on in da fields; ain't my bizniss."

The lieutenant began to become annoyed. "NOTHING seems to be word of choice around here, lately. Why were you all celebrating so passionately a few nights ago, Annette? The report we received from the steamboat river captain was quite explicit."

The woman gave out a bitter laugh. "All da white folks went away. Ain't dat reason enuff? We wuz free for da first time in our lives, and da Lord be praised for our deliverance!"

Shannon perked up; "Deliverance from WHAT, Annette?"

Her eyes closed to mere slits. "Why, I mean…from da white folks…like I said."

"I don't believe you. When an overseer leaves, another merely takes his place. It's really quite simple. This was not about white folks. This was about something far worse, wasn't it, Annette? Something that had you all frightened for your very souls."

"No! No!" the woman shrieked in panic. "I dont's know what you mean!" She stiffened, made a violent sign of the cross, and then rushed back into the mansion before either of the two men could stop her.

They looked at each other with a measure of satisfaction while Fuerst leaned back in his chair and slowly rocked back and forth, mulling over what had just transpired.

"Lieutenant, I firmly believe that we are on the right track. It would appear that we are learning more from the actions of these people than from their words, wouldn't you say?

This is not just about fear of retribution for the butchering of brutal white men who were most likely disposed of into the Mississippi. Had that been the case, someone out of the 80 or so slaves living here would have come forward and secretly told you who committed the murders prior to my arrival to curry favor, yes?"

"I can't argue with anything you've said, captain. There IS something far more sinister involved here. Jacques Dumaine's disappearance, or perhaps destruction is a better word, has not slackened their fears.

They are concerned with...another similar problem, I would imagine. It's almost as though they fear whatever might have left will return...to wreak havoc."

"Just come flat out and say it, man. Say that you think there was more than one vampire hidden away at this plantation."

The lieutenant stared at him intently and pursed his lips. "That was the rumor, sir. It would appear that at the very least, the slaves believe it too. As to its accuracy, well, we can bandy that back and forth after we've completed our investigation."

Shannon continued. "Captain, this afternoon I have sent for one more person who I thought you might be interested in seeing. I know you would like to have some food and get settled in, but this man offers an interesting perspective in that he is a trusted field hand. I have a hunch we should be able to obtain some valuable information from him. Speak o' the devil, here is comes now."

A huge hulk of a man dressed in rags lumbered out from behind the house and made his way up the front steps. He wore a floppy hat, which he removed when he stood before the officers. To no one's surprise, he was nervous, as evidenced by the wringing of the hat in his hands, and his long, slow breaths. This was not going to be easy for him.

Shannon broke the silence. "Hello again, Portafoy; I'd like you to meet Captain Fuerst. He's come a long way, and would like to ask you a few questions." The slave nodded his head up and down as a sign of agreement, but his face portrayed a look of apprehension with a slight dash of surrender mixed in for good measure.

Fuerst's voice changed markedly to that of a more soothing tone. He sensed that this slave's answers could cut through the fog of innuendo and whispers that had reached all to way to his own Masonic Holland Lodge in New York City. The way to get at the truth hidden away in this man was with honey, not vinegar.

"Portafoy, I understand that you were born here, is that so?"

"Yessuh, it's true. I's born here some 30 odd years ago. Don't know fo' shur, but it's what my momma sez, suh. She's da one dat keeps track of dates n' such."

"I see; and how long have you worked out in the fields?"

"Oh, since I's bout 10, suh. You see, I wuz big fo' my age; they put me outside sooner den da othuh lil' boys."

"I have no doubt about that, my friend." The captain's soothing voice now changed to that of an almost pleading tone. "I hope that you will regard me as your friend, Portafoy. I am here on a very important mission, to help vanquish evil. You believe that there is evil in this world, don't you?"

"Why yessuh, I shur do; da bible sez so."

Fuerst beamed. "Excellent! Most excellent! It has recently come to our attention that you were of great help to a young gentleman from Pennsylvania who lived on this very plantation a short time ago, am I right?" The big man unconsciously shifted his feet as though wishing to leave.

"You recall the person to whom I am referring, do you not, Portafoy? I believe his name was...Larson, John Larson, a student from an agricultural college in the northeast."

Portafoy looked directly at the captain. "Dat's true; I helped him with some... tests...yes, lab tests he called em' suh; always diggin' up da dirt and puttin' it in some bottles. He said he wuz here to help make things grow better."

"I see; I've been told that you assisted him while he was here."

"Yessuh; I drove him round da plantation to da fields and fetched things fo' him...He shur wuz good to me. And we talked bout things, too."

"What became of this young man?" There was a sharp silence which seemed to increase with intensity as the seconds passed.

Fuerst was touching a raw nerve, but he knew he was getting close to the truth. "Let me ask you again, Portafoy. What became of this young man?"

The slave's voice grew weak. "Why, he...he died, suh."

"Yes, that is what we have been told by the local authorities. We're quite sure of THAT fact; what we want to know is HOW he died."

The reply was little more than a mumble. "He...dun drowned in da river out back, suh."

Fuerst's voice rose dramatically. "Is that what REALLY happened? Did John Larson drown in an unfortunate fishing accident, or was he MURDERED, Portafoy, murdered by a...MUMIANI?"

The Negro's head jerked upwards as he screamed in terror. "NOOOO! NOOOO! Pleez don't asks me more, suh!" He reached inside his trouser pocket and pulled out a string of white rosary beads complete with a small cross; then with shaking hands he placed then over his head and let the string hang like a necklace while he began to pray. "Da Lord...da Lord is my shepherd!"

Fuerst rammed home his point emphatically. "Jacques Dumaine was a MUMIANI, a VAMPIRE, wasn't he, Portafoy? The slaves rose up and KILLED him, but not before he attacked John Larson. Larson did not drown. He left the plantation as a night creature BEFORE Dumaine's destruction and is now free...free to roam and kill at will. Is that not the real truth?"

The poor wretch could endure no more. "YEEESSS! YEEESSS! We tried to warn him, tried to make him leave, but he wouldn't go. He wanted to bring back da' cane, suh, da' sugar cane. Den one night da master up an' took him, an it was too late. Dat's all I knows, suh. He up and left one night, an' we ain't never seen him since. Dat's da God's honest truth, suh, so help me."

Fuerst softened. "I believe you. Thank you very much for your help, Portafoy. I know this has not been easy, but you have performed a great service. By corroborating the rumors that we have heard, it might now be possible to track this creature down and destroy it. Remember what the holy bible says; in the end, good must triumph over evil. You may go."

The Negro went down the stairs, glancing repeatedly at both men as he descended. "Don't lets him come back here, suh. If he finds out what dun happened to da master, he'll kill us all... or worse. Dat's why we all so scared, suh, scared bout the mumiani comin' back to da' plantation."

When he reached solid ground, he broke out into a fast trot towards the direction of the slave shacks and never looked back. Shannon watched him with great satisfaction.

"Well, captain, congratulations are in order. It appears that you have uncovered the truth. I have a number of other people scheduled to meet with you tonight, but honestly, I don't know how much more we actually need."

Fuerst nodded slowly in agreement, but was sad nonetheless. "Portafoy has confirmed the rumors that we had hoped were nothing more than superstitious slave talk. The other reported incident of the murdered AWOL troopers right after the fall of Vicksburg by this Jacques Dumaine now must be considered fact, rather than the ramblings of drunken fools."

He clapped his hands together. "The pieces of the puzzle can now be put together. We know the escaped creature's name, we have its description, and we received word from the Agricultural College of Pennsylvania that this student John Larson was from York, Pennsylvania.

When you combine all of the above with the reports coming out of Gettysburg by our fellow Masons, I can safely say with a fair amount of certainty that we also know the creature's location."

"I agree completely, captain. We are...**on the square**. What are your orders?"

"Wait until after the evening interviews, and then report back to your **mother**. I shall do likewise. We must eradicate this filth before it has further opportunities to kill or spread its disease to others."

Shannon raised his eyes to the sky, and in a hushed voice uttered the words "**So Mote It Be**."

CHAPTER 5

A Family Visit

As dusk arrived, John flipped open the trap door to the roof of the Cemetery Gatehouse and took a deep breath. The air continued to be fouled by smells left over from the recent battle, but that was more a hindrance than repulsion for him. It meant that he would still be unable to detect the distinct odor of the Freemasons.

A valuable tool of early warning was no longer at his disposal, forcing him to rely solely on sight and intuition. With so many of those adversaries interspersed amongst the civilians and soldiers remaining in the town and surrounding area, the odds were not in his favor. He hoped that the Federal Freemason survivor of the previous week's attack on him would be unable to rally support for a hunt.

Perhaps with so many other things going on—cleaning up the town, care of the wounded, rounding up Rebel stragglers, and burying the dead, they would be spread far too thin. But then again, perhaps they had placed his destruction at the top of their list. John was sure that the latter course of action was even now being implemented. They were, after all, so predictable.

He could not linger much longer in Gettysburg; one or two days at the most to pick up any additional information before turning west to track down the tattered Army of Northern Virginia. Another series of select attacks upon their command structure might produce a devastating effect on Lee's ability to launch another invasion of the North; that could trigger a series of defensive battles for the great commander, something John was sure Lee would be loath to consider in view of his combative nature.

John decided against walking to the diamond this evening. Instead, he would concentrate on garnering information from Baltimore Street itself, and what better choice to start than the house of the Garlachs, his own cousins. It was here that he had stayed for several summers while he worked in Gettysburg. It was also the place he had chosen as his first place of refuge during the three day battle; there he had hidden safely under the back porch.

As he reached their residence, he quickly scanned the exterior of the two story building, and although it was dark, he saw minor evidence of battle damage to the red bricks and mortar, most probably Union rifle fire. He wondered what could be said for his relatives inside, particularly his favorite cousins, youngsters Anna and William. Had they been hurt, and what about other townspeople caught in the midst of the two clashing armies? Surely there must have been scores of civilian casualties.

Suddenly John realized that he was under scrutiny. A Union soldier was eyeing him from a first floor parlor window. Could the damned Freemasons have somehow found out about this location and set up a lookout, hoping for his eventual return? They knew full well that night creatures kept multiple resting places as a safeguard against eventual discovery.

Perhaps they were systematically hunting down and cleansing the spots; that most certainly meant the warehouse on Railroad Street where he had his little skirmish with the Masons the week before was being faithfully watched from dusk until dawn.

Yes, faithfully, John thought to himself with disgust. He hated the self-righteous attitude of these secular holy men.

They had hunted down his kind all over the world for hundreds of years, all in the name of almighty God, of course. Yet they had no problems invoking help from the same God as they butchered each another in fruitless wars.

And what could be more fruitless than the war they were undertaking at this very moment? Brother against brother, father against son, neighbor against neighbor.

Why was their God not putting a stopping to it? He glanced up to the sky with a look of disdain and muttered "Where is my answer? And what have I done to deserve this fate?"

He waited, staring up at the stars, but there was no reply; "Just as I expected." The drawing of the curtains in the window snapped him back to his perilous situation. The soldier was gone. The only way of knowing what that meant was to either eavesdrop or sneak a quick peek inside the room.

The latter scenario was out of the question. The chance of a dead John Larson being recognized by his relatives was not in his best interests. But the glowing hurricane lamps were the next best thing to sight. They provided outlined silhouettes through the thin curtains, and he was able to take full advantage.

The soldier appeared in no great hurry to leave the house and report his findings. In fact, he was on a bed in the front parlor, resting in an upright position. A stocky woman was assisting him by placing pillows between his back and the headboard, while another man was standing patiently nearby with a tray of food.

John immediately recognized the shadowy figures as those of his older cousins, Catherine Garlach, and her husband Henry.

This was no vengeful Freemason on guard duty. Rather, it was a convalescing soldier under the care of loyal United States citizens trying to help in any possible way. John smiled; how like her. The last time he found a Union soldier under Catherine's protection, the circumstances were quite different.

It was well over a week ago, during the close of the first day's fighting. John discovered a frightened Union general, of all people, hiding in the family's combination woodshed/pigsty. He had to summon all of his self-control to stop from throttling the shameless officer into the next world. He disgraced the uniform.

Now that THIS soldier's situation had been determined, John decided to listen in on whatever loose talk he could decipher. But the front of the house was no place for that. It was much too conspicuous, and he still had to pay heed to civilians and military personnel moving about on foot and horseback, particularly those bastards trying to hunt him down.

No, the best place for him was on the side of the house, in the darkness of the alley leading to the back yard. There was virtually no light between the narrow houses on Baltimore Street, and with his enhanced sense of hearing, he would have little problem picking up any voices within.

Once he found a spot to his liking, he merely sat on a cracker barrel in the darkness and listened in on the conversation going on in the house. Catherine's voice was the first to be heard.

"Well, captain, I must say the color has definitely returned to your face. When you arrived here, you were so ashen and weak. To tell the truth, I feared for your life. Don't you think he looks much better today, Henry?"

"Without question, without question, my dear; you certainly have a healer's touch. Now that you are comfortable, captain, it is high time for a late supper, and here it is. Nothing heavy, mind you, but my wife has made some fine noodle soup to go along with the bread and butter. I trust you appetite has returned?"

The officer replied gratefully; "I feel as though I could devour enough food for an entire brigade, sir; that's a natural fact. And I cannot tell you how grateful I am that you and your wife have so freely invited me into your home while I..." The man's voice slowly trailed off; "recover."

There was a long, heavy pause, followed by Catherine in a more softened tone. "Captain, do you feel well enough to tell us how you happened to lose your leg? Of course, if you'd rather not, we understand perfectly."

"Not at all, ma'am; I have no objection. Somehow, I get the distinct impression that I will be telling this particular story over and over again for a great many years. From my own experience, I have to say that it's hard to ignore a missing limb." The Garlachs laughed uneasily as though unsure to agree with him.

"So many of my comrades lost them...limbs that is, that whenever I'd visit any of them for the first time, my eyes would just seem to end up staring at the missing part. I guess we're so used to seeing two arms and two legs that anything less seems almost freakish, do you know what I mean?"

John did not hear a reply, but he was sure the silence was a nod of affirmation from both Catherine and John to continue.

"Well, here goes; about two o'clock on the afternoon of the second days fighting, the regiment was ordered forward a short distance and took position in line of battle on a woody knoll a few hundred yards to the left of a peach orchard, facing in the direction of the Emmitsburg Road. I observed the enemy's skirmishers advancing through the fields beyond the road, and almost at the same time Union skirmishers in the peach orchard moved out to meet them.

A brisk fire was at once opened, the shots of the enemy coming so uncomfortably near us that we deemed it prudent to seek shelter of the woods to await orders. We did not have long to wait, for the movement of the skirmishers was immediately followed by the advance of the enemy's main lines, consisting of General Longstreet's corps, and the rattle of musketry began upon our right.

Noticing an unoccupied wheat field to our left, forming a wide gap between the flanks of our brigade and the right of another, our brigade commander, Colonel DeTrobriand, ordered the 17th Maine to occupy it. The regiment immediately moved double quick through the woods in our front, across the wheat field to a stone wall separating it from some thick woods beyond, which we found occupied by the enemy. They opened heavy musket fire upon us as we neared the wall.

But upon reaching it we were well protected and had no difficulty in holding our position against repeated assaults. Our movement into the wheat field was soon followed by a similar one on the part of a Pennsylvania regiment, the 110th, if I remember correctly, that was directed to connect with our right. It necessitated advancing through a ravine under severe fire.

Lacking the friendly shelter of the stone wall which barely extended to the right of our line, that regiment was unable to withstand the terrific fire poured upon it, and soon retired with the loss of many of its members." The lieutenant paused for a moment, presumably to take a drink, John speculated, and then continued.

"Taking advantage of the repulse of the 110th, the enemy advanced into the ravine evidently with the intention of flanking the 17th Maine. As soon as that was discovered, a portion of our right was ordered to swing back at right angles with the stone wall in front, and it was my duty to communicate that order to the captains of several companies, as the rattle of musketry and roar of artillery from a battery near us prevented the voice of our commander being heard along the line.

This movement was promptly executed in the face of severe fire from the enemy in front and upon our flank, but with heavy losses to the regiment, as many men fell under the shower of bullets. The attempt of the enemy was frustrated for the time being, and the regiment held its position until the ammunition gave out, when it retired across the wheat field over a ridge in the rear into a narrow road by the side of a belt of woods, where it halted, reformed, and was resupplied with ammunition."

There was another pause, followed by an almost self-conscious tone. "Excuse me being so specific, but the events are seared into my memory. I do not wish to be bombastic or worse, to bore you; do you want me to continue?"

"Please go on, captain," Catherine pleaded. "The bravery and sacrifice of our boys needs to be told, especially by those who were there sharing the dangers."

"All right then. Where was I? Oh yes. About this time, General Birney and several of his staff road along the line, and observing the enemy advancing toward a Federal battery near our left in the vicinity of the rocky area that I believe you residents call the Devil's Den, turned to the 17th Maine and directed it to move forward while he accompanied it in person into the wheat field where we had passed a few moments before.

Here we were ordered to halt in the open field on what we supposed to be the new line of battle then being formed. While the regiment occupied this exposed position in full view of the enemy, I was struck in the right leg above the knee by a bullet with such force as to throw me upon my face. Colonel Merrill, who was standing near me, immediately cut one of the straps from his sword belt and bound it tightly around my limb to stop the flow of blood."

The captain halted his tale for a few moments, as though remembering the intense pain the wound had caused him, but he collected his thoughts and finished.

"He ordered four men near at hand to take me to the rear in a rubber blanket, as the stretchers of the ambulance corps were all in use at that moment. From this time my personal knowledge of the moments of the regiment ceased.

I was conveyed to what at that time was presumed to be a safe distance from the front, where I met the assistant surgeon of the regiment, who examined my wound and gave it such attention as circumstance would permit. Later in the afternoon, I was removed with others farther back into the woods to a place of safety where the division hospital was established.

On the afternoon of the following day, my wound was carefully examined by our regimental surgeon, Doctor Hersom, and upon his recommendation, my limb was amputated. I remained in the field hospital for several days until Sergeant Berry from our ambulance corps was able to secure accommodations here in your house...but of course you already know Sergeant Berry.

Well, that is about it; my leg is gone, but I am now in excellent care, and I hope not to be a burden to you or your family for too much longer,"

Henry spoke up; "The honor is ours, captain. You may stay with our family for as long as it takes your wound to properly heal. I believe that the combination of my wife's doting, regular visits from the army doctors, and provisions from the Sanitary Commission will put you on the road to a full recovery."

"I have no absolutely doubts about it, sir. You have made me feel like a part of your family, and I have only been here a few days." Now the captain's voice changed to an almost mischievous tone. "By the way, I understand that you had some visitors this afternoon, am I right?"

Henry hemmed and hawed, as though embarrassed by the question. "Why, yes, two gentlemen did happen to stop by today for some...carpentry work they needed done."

"Well, I have heard that you are a very talented cabinet maker, sir. But I fail to see why two soldiers would have need of a cabinet. Could it be that it was something a bit larger, almost man-sized?"

John was totally perplexed by this line of questioning, and it piqued his interest. Henry exhaled and sounded almost sheepish. "All right, captain; the soldiers paid me to build a coffin for their commanding officer so that he can be transported home in a proper manner. I did not want it known so as not to disturb you."

A hearty laugh resounded through the parlor. "When you have cheated death as I have, it becomes hard to be disturbed by anything other than actual battle. Build away to your heart's content, my good man, by all means. I reckon that your services will be required on more than just this one occasion. Unfortunately, many loved ones will be seeking to bring their brave boys home."

He gave a heartfelt plea. "But please, call me Charles so that I in turn may call you Henry and Catherine. That is my one and only request."

Henry replied quickly. "And it shall be fulfilled; what do you say, my good wife?"

"But of course; we shall get through this difficult time together, and be all the stronger for it, so help us God."

A short pause was followed by a group "Amen." John rolled his eyes and exhaled. "Oh sure...The Almighty will help you; all right people, no need to get maudlin in there."

While the conversation was interesting, it provided little useful information, other than that houses throughout Gettysburg were possibly filled with convalescing soldiers from both sides. He could tell by the red towels and tablecloths hung out to indicate just that fact.

John was hoping for something more substantial. He would reconnoiter the town a bit further. Soon it would be time to move on.

He continued down Baltimore Street a short way until he got to the corner of Breckinridge on his left, and then froze. His senses warned that he was being watched once again, this time from someone lurking in the shadows. If it was merely a Freemason lookout, he would have no problem dealing with a lone adversary, as long as the man was unable to sound the alarm.

However, before John could turn to confront him, the stranger spoke like a carnival barker from out of the darkness. "You look to me like a young man who knows a real bargain when he sees one. Am I right, or am I right?" John withdrew from attack mode and flashed an evil sneer that went undetected. This was anyone but a Freemason.

"That would of course depend on what you're selling, friend. Do you think you have what I need...what I...REALLY need?"

The man responded with the speed of a Gatling gun. "I have a little bit of everything here at my disposal. But I've forgotten my manners, haven't I? Let me introduce myself; the name's Chris Matthews, at your service. I'm a purveyor of fine things old and new."

John was beginning to feel hungry AND annoyed; a bad combination for a blathering salesman. "I have just the baubles a young man of your ilk could use to impress the folks back home, know what I mean, hah? Take a gander at these little beauties."

He bent down and slowly lifted the lid of a wooden cedar chest. It took only a moment for John to realize how the cretin had come by the items. There were pocket knives and watches of all shapes and sizes, along with a variety of smoking pipes and tobacco pouches. The man puffed up as though truly proud of his wares.

"What do you think now, eh? This is a fine collection to choose from, if I do say so myself, and I do." He slapped his hands together. "Now, let's get down to business, what interests you tonight?"

John began to smolder. He clenched his jaw and pursed his lips together tightly, barely able to give a reply. "What interests me is just where, and more importantly, HOW did you acquire these...little beauties?"

He stepped closer to the man, who completely mistook the movement to be one of interest. "Let's not quibble. I feel disposed to say that they were merely lying about here and there, know what I mean, hah?"

John cocked his head and stepped even closer. "They were lying about here and there on the battlefield, weren't they? You stripped the dead of the only reminders left on this earth that they were once men...husbands, fathers, brothers. This does not bother you?"

"Well, that depends on whose property it is. You see, I have the posters memorized. They say: Citizens visiting the battlefield are warned against carrying away any government property, and all those having taken such property, either Federal or Confederate, are directed to return the same without delay, to my office in Gettysburg, thereby saving themselves from arrest and punishment; signed W. Willard Smith, Acting Provost Marshall."

The hawker actually appeared proud of his recital. "You see, what I have here is not government property, but really private property of a sort, so no need to be high and mighty about the whole affair. These things ain't doing them no good no more, that's for sure.

Why waste them? Why let them get buried along with the stiffs? And let's not forget, it wasn't easy retrieving these items, not by a long shot what with the sights and smells. It's a hard world, my lad, and the sooner you realize that the better off you'll be."

John quickly grabbed the man by the throat with both hands and began to squeeze, lightly at first to experience some fun, and then harder while the wretch flailed about and gasped for air. There was a look of astonishment on his reddening face as he was pushed backwards into the shadows.

John smiled a toothy grin and explained the situation. "I realize that it will be a BETTER world when you have departed it, know what I mean, hah? You are the lowest of the low, and do not deserve to live."

The man soon passed out with a final gurgle, and his hands dropped to his sides while John kept him propped up. "You will at least do one good deed, my ghoulish friend. You will furnish me great satisfaction before you die."

That said, John unceremoniously smacked the ghoul's head to one side, then bit down into his neck and began to suck deeply for several exquisite moments, only to stop.

"No, no, no. I will not kill you THIS way. I do not relish the prospect of bumping into you for the next several hundred years. I never want to see you AGAIN."

With that, John balled up his fist and punched the man's face half way through to the back of the skull. It would appear to all that this was a robbery attempt gone very badly.

The deceased Mr. Matthews fell in a heap, forcing the contents of the cedar chest to overturn and spill out all over the ground. As John stood licking his hand, he felt that strange, cold blast of air once again on his back. It was accompanied by an even colder sounding voice.

"Ahhh, Larson…glad to see that you haven't lost your sense of justice."

CHAPTER 6

Death Returns

John turned to face an innocuous looking man of about 30, roughly dressed, with a medium build, and brown eyes that matched his hair; in short, a person who would not be given a second glance unless he happened to run into a church service naked. Yet as John's fear rose, he knew that this was no ordinary person. In fact, he was not a person at all.

"DEATH…you are still here I see, although I must say that when last we met, that night along the Emmitsburg Road, you had the look of a tattered Rebel soldier."

The reply to John's statement was quick yet nonchalant. "I take any form I choose to perform my task. Although the battle is over, there is still much work to be done, not only here in the town but the outlying areas as well."

"That's right; you must be reaping a very rich harvest these days. So it was you I heard the other night when I was outside the chur…"

John was stopped in mid-sentence by a cruel, laughing reply. "Go ahead, finish up; weren't you about to say outside the church in the alleyway enjoying a sumptuous meal fit for a KING?"

John stiffened. "I don't see any point in continuing this conversation. Why don't you just go your way, and I'll go mine? It is obvious that we both have our own particular...work to do."

The being stepped forward, forcing John to instinctively step back to keep a safe distance once he felt the cold. "I am here to end the suffering of those whose life force is all but spent so that they may pass unfettered to the next dimension. It is a kind and noble duty that I have faithfully performed since time immemorial.

But why do YOU remain here? Did I not tell you once before that your abominations have not gone unnoticed?"

John thundered; "WHAT abominations? I have chosen to aid the most glorious nation on the face of the earth. I am here to gather any information possible so that I can continue to strike the Rebels where it matters most, in their leadership. With their generals disabled, the rest will be nothing more than frightened sheep."

There was a short pause. "And since you brought it up, are you going to assist the low life bastard that I just happily smashed to pieces?"

The reply became cool and distant, but with a marked tinge of irritation. "You TOTALLY misunderstand; I do not help those who have no SOUL. For the likes of HIM, there is only...oblivion. That will be your fate too, IF you make the wrong choice; but I sense that somehow, in the end...you will not."

John gave a bewildered look. "CHOICE? CHOICE? What the hell are you babbling about?"

Death stepped closer. "The Vampire Council is gathering to convene because of YOU, yet you remain here...defiant. Despite obtaining the results in battle that you had hoped for, your actions have helped to alter the course of this war, and perhaps even the history of the world itself.

You should have followed the code of the night creature and targeted only the dregs and scum of society. Now defeat for the South is a very distinct possibility. For this you will be punished…and SEVERELY."

"I know nothing of this council you speak of, but if the time comes I will state my case before them and be vindicated. And now I must be off; there are still things to learn before I go back on the attack. Lee's army is a wounded but still dangerous animal. It cannot be allowed to refit and re-supply for a renewal of hostilities against my country."

"Night creature, you have no conception of what lies in store for you." John brazenly turned his back and continued down Baltimore Street, taunting Death as he went.

"What, no final words of wisdom or great import?" When there was no answer, he glanced back over his shoulder. His personal Greek Chorus was gone. John yelled out into the night "GOOD RIDDANCE!"

He soon remembered something Henry Garlach had mentioned to the lieutenant, a Sanitary Commission of some sort. That would most certainly be one of those outside agencies; plenty of loose talk could be had there. All he needed was to find out where it was. Asking townspeople was too dangerous; that left the military, but how was he to know if they were Freemasons when they could not be smelled beforehand?

As John was passing East High Street, the screams of a woman could be heard. "Help me! Somebody please help! Murder! MURRRDERRR!

He gave out a short chuckle. "It certainly did not take very long for the late Mr. Matthews to be discovered; identified will be another story."

The sounds of galloping horses were soon heard coming from the direction of the diamond. There was a fair sized group that by all appearances was heading towards the direction of the crime scene, but John wondered if that was its true purpose. He felt an uneasy feeling as the riders swiftly passed by, and when he shot them a furtive glance he understood why.

This was no provost guard bent on restoring order in the streets, although to the naked eye they were undoubtedly Union soldiers. It was the very nature of their weapons that indicated this was actually a troop of elite Freemasons stalkers searching for a night creature; searching for HIM.

Besides the standard issue Spenser carbine, the riders had amongst their possessions crossbows, axes, and pikes, while a silver cross dangled loosely over each saddle horn. Any of the aforementioned items could cause John considerable grief.

If he had to defend against all of those weapons, the Vampire Council would be the least of his worries.

He hoped that the gory sight of the faceless Mr. Matthews might throw off the investigators, but if any Freemasons were sharp enough to notice the small bite marks on the man's neck, that would be akin to striking the mother lode. It would provide undisputed proof that a night creature still remained in Gettysburg; if only he had not stumbled upon that cursed corpse robber!

John felt it would be prudent to put as much distance between him and the stalkers as possible without arousing suspicion. As he quickened his pace, he arrived at the corner of Middle Street, and Fahnestock Brothers Dry Goods Store; only the store bore little resemblance to the quiet shop one went to buy anything from carpenter's nails to ladies dress materials. The store was overflowing with people and crates that stretched out the front entrance to the sidewalk itself.

Of course, John thought; THIS is the location of the Sanitary Commission. Despite the evening hour, there was still a bustle of activity inside and out. Women with clip boards checked off lists, soldiers packed boxes onto waiting carts, and clerks waited on both customers and hospital staffers looking to pick up valuable medical supplies.

John knew that entering the store was out of the question. There was a good possibility that at least one of the Fahnestock brothers was hovering about the establishment, and he could not afford to be recognized, especially with the stalkers nearby. So he stood across the street, contently taking in the sights and sounds of this new establishment. It seemed odd to him how many women were engaged in the trafficking of the precious goods.

Furthermore, they appeared to be in near complete control of the bustling situation, even directing dismayed teamsters and soldiers. John set to musing; perhaps the war could provide opportunities for women that were never dreamt of before, and why not?

After all, they seemed to him always to be much more organized and efficient than men, not to mention a hell of a lot cleaner. Their temperament was also much less explosive. The fire eaters and abolitionists who started the war could take a few lessons in compassion and understanding from them, to be sure.

He watched with fascination as one woman in particular seemed to stand out above all the others. She appeared to be in her early 50's, with a medium build and straw-like graying hair. Her most prominent feature, strangely enough, was a sparsely outlined moustache that could not possibly be missed in a mirror.

But it was not her appearance that made her stand out, but rather her voice. Whenever someone tried to get her attention away from what she was doing, if only for a moment, she would raise a hand, shake her head quickly from side to side and whine "NOT NOWWWW!"

The voice sounded worse than that of a bleating calf, and caused all those around her to quietly slip away in defeat. One clerk had just left with a shrug and drooped shoulders as she returned to her task of checking a bill of lading from a teamster who had brought up supplies for the wounded by cart from the railroad station.

"All right now," she said. "Let me finish this inventory." The teamster made the mistake of speaking up; "You stopped at the canned oysters, lady."

"I KNOW where I left off," she barked, it was at the DRIED FRUIT, and my name is Dorothy…Miss Dorothy Smith; that leaves…25 boxes of catsup, 300 loaves of bread, and 50 cases of concentrated milk, courtesy of Mr. Borden himself all the way from Brewster, New York, I do believe. Just let me get a head count on that for a moment."

The teamster now stood as dutifully as a scolded student sent to the corner to reflect on his misdeeds. All he could do as he waited for her tally was to twirl his hat in his hand; he dared not do more. Finally, she finished her numeric mumbling and made the announcement.

"This is fine; everything is in order. You may go back now for the medical supplies. I just received word that they are arriving at Hanover Junction."

"Hold it there a minute, lady…I mean…Miss Smith. It's nearly 10:00 o'clock, an' I been drivin' this stinkin' cart back and forth for five straight hours. I'll be damned if…" He was unceremoniously cut off, and cut down.

"You'll be damned if you don't go down to the junction and get those medical supplies; there's quinine, digitalis, laudanum, ammonia water, and all manner of items the hospital doctors need RIGHT NOW! While you have been sitting on your rump, brave soldiers have been suffering. Now…what shall it be?"

The man cocked his head and shot her a look of surprised admiration. "Miss Smith, I'll be damned if you don't make perfect sense." He sighed and turned to climb back up on his cart. "I'll be back in a bit with the medicine…ma'am."

Dorothy smiled broadly and responded sweetly as though there had been no altercation. "Thank you so much, Mr. Murphy. I simply knew in my heart that you would not let the boys down."

John was mesmerized by the entertaining vignette, but it did nothing to clarify the situation at hand. He felt he still needed more information before setting out after Lee's army; and there was something else he needed—more blood.

He was unable to quench his thirst with Mr. Matthews, and the amputated limbs from the night before had merely whet his appetite. COPIOUS amounts of blood were needed, and soon, as he was beginning to weaken. Perhaps he could locate another "undesirable" in town and whisk him away to the woods, where he could safely enjoy his meal in peace and quiet.

Was that too much to ask for? As John passed Fahnestock's and continued down Baltimore Street, he noticed two pretty young ladies strolling up from the diamond on the opposite side of the street. They held embroidered silk kerchiefs, which they occasionally placed close to their noses, undoubtedly containing perfume in an effort to drive away the stench of the night air.

Their dresses were simple, but a nicely colored light blue and green, respectively. Between them was a rather handsome young man, who, despite his sleepy eyed look, seemed quite content in his present situation of having a lady on each arm. John recognized the girls as locals, but could not readily recall their names; the young man was a stranger, with his left arm in a sling.

But this was no civilian; he was a soldier, and a Confederate to boot. Despite the distance between them, John could detect a slight southern twang in his speech as he bantered with his female companions. But it was the topic of the conversation that left no doubt as to where the young man swore his allegiance.

The definitive proof came in the form of a question from one of the ladies. "Oh my, Henry, I had no idea that you were a staff officer of the late General Jackson. Newspapers here in the North did not quite know what to make of him. Do you happen to have any stories of the general?"

"Why, yes, I do," he replied with amusement, "and there is one or two that I might actually be able to tell you."

The trio laughed together as if on cue until the girls grew silent while they waited expectantly for their handsome bard to regale them with fanciful tales. The officer looked the picture of concentration for several moments. He knew that any story needed to fit his present company, and that was no easy task. Suddenly his face beamed with a spark of recollection.

"Of course! Well, there was this one time earlier in the war while we were in the valley...the Shenandoah Valley, that is, when we rode passed a fine persimmon tree simply chock full of the luscious fruit. Now the general had a soft spot for certain fruits, so he naturally calls a halt and proceeds to climb the tree.

As you may know, the best fruit is usually the hardest to reach, so the general climbs up a ways." The girls nodded in agreement but said nothing so as not to break the mood. "He decides on a good spot, then proceeds to pick and devour the sweet persimmons like a famished little farm boy.

When he's finally had his fill, he naturally attempts to go down the same way he went up, but gets completely tangled up in the limbs, and won't budge an inch further. We had to tie some nearby fence rails together and use them as a ramp so he could slide down. It was all we could do to keep from falling to the ground laughing."

The girls squealed in delight. There was nothing like privileged information, whether it was important or trivial was of no consequence. The fact that they knew something others did not made them feel special. The green dressed girl piped up. "Oh, Henry, that was wonderful, and you told it soooo well. Please go on!"

The little band continued down the street, perhaps to a tavern, John surmised. He could not understand how Rebel prisoners were allowed to stroll about the town. What was to prevent them from attempting to escape, and how did it look that Union soldiers recuperating from wounds were in hospital beds while the men who gave them those wounds were gallivanting about the town with Union women?

These were indeed strange times to live in. But then again, John reasoned, he was no longer alive, and he had to have blood this night. One would think with so many soldiers and civilians scattered about Gettysburg, he would be able to find a decent derelict for dinner.

But blood would have to wait once more. The sounds of pounding hoofs thundered in his direction, the very sounds he had heard when the Freemason stalkers flew by earlier in the evening. John reached the center of town and ran to the doorway of attorney David Wills' house, located on the southeast corner of the square. The door was locked, but the recessed entrance way provided just enough darkness for him to remain hidden.

Unfortunately, the stalkers numbers had increased. The original troop stopped just short of York Street, while another troop thundered from the opposite direction on Carlyle Street. The grassy diamond appeared to be their rendezvous point.

John counted 14 Freemasons in all, with every one of them sporting the lethal weaponry he had seen earlier. Could there possibly be any MORE of these sons of bitches riding around the town, and what of the outlying areas?

While his situation was precarious, it nonetheless afforded John an unexpectedly splendid opportunity to listen in on their impromptu war council. Perhaps he could stay a step ahead of them for another day and get his bearings for another strike against the secessionists...or perhaps he could be discovered and justly sent to the depths of hell like the soulless thing that he was. After all, wasn't it all in one's point of view?

CHAPTER 7

The Freemasons Close In

T he two troops gathered in the diamond, staying atop their sweaty, panting horses while conferring with one another. The talk was fast and furious, with urgent inquiries firing back and forth until one soldier from the group raised an axe and shouted them all down.

Up to now, John was unable to discern anything due to their simultaneous discussions, but as the officer prepared to speak, this looked like the opportunity he had hoped for.

"All right, men; we now know for certain that this creature is STILL in Gettysburg. The body of that corpse robber up the street has confirmed our suspicions. The bite mark on the dead man's neck is the actual proof we needed." There followed a general grumbling of affirmation and head nodding.

"And now I can ALSO tell you with a fair amount of certainty that this creature's name is John Larson, formerly from nearby York. Vital intelligence newly received by telegraph from our brother members in Louisiana has confirmed persistent rumors of a long time nest of this filth hidden away on an isolated sugar cane plantation."

John was dumbstruck; his cloak of anonymity had been torn away in a flash. "Eyewitness information has been conflicting, but by day after tomorrow the latest, we shall have a physical description of this creature; that should give us the edge we need to track him down, wherever he may be."

He then lowered his voice markedly, almost as though he were ashamed of what he was about to say. "That edge will be sharpened with the arrival of the... Dhampir."

The troopers looked at each other with a mixture of amazement and disgust. They appeared to be uncomfortable with the leader's startling announcement. A blue rider in the back of the group quickly shouted out.

"We do not need, nor do we ask, for THAT kind of help; send it back where it came from!" The group let out a resounding belch of agreement, but the leader sat stone-faced on his horse, waiting patiently for the noise to subside while he waived his hand in objection.

"The orders are quite explicit, with no room for personal interpretation. We are to make use of this...tracker...for as long as it takes us to accomplish our mission. THAT is where we must focus our energy, on the mission, not the means. It is our sacred duty."

The troopers quieted down, mulling over the words of their leader with obvious distaste, as evidenced by the many sour expressions of forced resignation. But those expressions paled when compared to the look of astonishment on John's face.

He was still in a state of near shock over the discovery of his identity. Just how extensive was this Freemason network? Was there no place he could now count on for safety?

The leader continued. "Men, let us continue our holy quest. Half of us will remain here to scour the area, while the rest shall take the York Road to search this creature's birthplace. Let us be off. May the Supreme Being guide us on the proper path; **SO MOTE IT BE!**"

With a lusty huzzah the group split up as directed; one troop went down Chambersburg Street, while the other doubled back on Baltimore Street headed towards the York Road. In a few moments, all was silent, save for a smattering of town residents left scratching their heads as to what had just transpired in their very midst.

John remained leaning against the Wills' front door, and suddenly felt a chill. The seriousness of the situation had escalated to an alarming level. He did not get an opportunity to think about those questions, as a voice jolted him from out of the darkness of the entrance way.

"You're in a bit of a pickle, aren't you, John?" It was the voice of Death, who was now somehow standing right beside him. "Lady Luck does seem to have deserted you, at least up to a point; but she's like that, you know. You can never depend on her when you really need her the most."

If John still had a working heart, it would have skipped a beat. As it was, he exhaled loudly and turned to square off with his agitator. "Don't you have anything better to do? Isn't anyone DYING right now?"

"Not at the moment, at least not anyone who DESERVES my help. I should think that you would be on your way, now that you have been awarded privileged information on a silver platter."

John shrugged his shoulders. "I can deal with being unmasked, and the additional Freemasons are just another inconvenience. Besides, these bumblers may get in other's way."

Death scowled. "I'm not referring to the Freemasons, idiot. IT has been sent for, and when it arrives, you will be relentlessly hunted down and summarily dispatched to…well…now is not the time to quibble about THOSE details."

John whined with disgust. "What is all this IT business? First the Freemasons, and now you; can't any of you come up with an actual name?"

Death shook his head. "You ignorant fool. You honestly don't know, do you? It is now painfully obvious that you were not properly instructed by your master prior to your departure from Louisiana. This is a glaring deficiency that may cost you dearly."

"I left the plantation prematurely of my own free will to aid the Union cause. You are aware of that at least. Now tell me what it is I am supposed to fear."

There was a long pause before his bold mandate was answered, as though John's brashness had caught Death off guard. "Did you not hear the troop leader say the word... Dhampir?"

John was puzzled. "I did hear him say something. I was not quite sure what he said, to be honest; that is why I could not understand the reaction of the other Freemasons. I have never heard that word uttered before, so I can't know what it means, or be frightened by it either, now can I?"

"Oh, but you really should; a Dhampir is very much akin to say...a mulatto, a half breed, a freak of nature. But that does not truly describe it or the severity of your own situation. A Dhampir is half human, AND half vampire. Its' kind has been used, mostly in Eastern Europe, for hundreds of years, for the express purpose of tracking down vampires and killing them."

The tone grew ominous. "Unfortunately for you, it also possesses many of the vampires' unique powers. Tales have often been said around the campfire that a vampire cannot evade capture and destruction once a Dhampir has picked up its trail."

John's felt his face beginning to tighten. "If it is HALF vampire, then why should it come after me? I am no threat to it."

The statement brought a crude laugh along with a measured reply. "That answer is quite simple, you see. The human half of the Dhampir is enraged by what has been done to it by the vampire, and so uses the added powers in its quest of destruction as a final, insulting gesture."

A lengthy pause followed. "That is very ironic, don't you think? It would appear that a Dhampir has been summoned by the Freemasons and is on its way from the Baltic region as we speak. For your sake, I hope its journey has only just begun."

John now rattled off questions fast and furiously. "How will I know when it's here? Will I feel its presence? What does they look like? Are they all the same?"

Death remained calm. "It does look human enough, except for the facial features, which tend be quite repulsive, even by my standards, which are decidedly low, by the way. Some of them have no nose, some actually have a bat's face; it can vary widely, to be honest" Then Death did something very uncharacteristic and cracked a wisp of a smile in the dark.

"But whatever this Dhampir happens to look like, you should have no problem picking it out of a crowded room. Of course, by that time it would probably be too late, I'm afraid."

"I'm glad to see that you're having such a good time," John spit out in disgust, and then he swooned, steadying himself against the front door.

"I have to feed; once that is out of the way, I will be able to think things out properly."

"Well, you've certainly come to the right place in that regard, and I may even be of some assistance. Do you see that storefront several doors down from the inn? I firmly believe that you will be able to attend to your...particular needs quite nicely there."

John was unconvinced. "How can you be so certain, and why have you suddenly decided to help me now? How do I know this isn't this some sort of trick?"

Death sounded almost embarrassed in the reply. "The truth be told, I have of late become interested in your particular…situation, so to speak, and I am intrigued as to how this will all play out."

John was incredulous. "You mean you don't KNOW? Even YOU don't know?"

The reply was cold and stiff, as though responding to an insult. "That is correct; there are many variables that can alter the outcome of events. The future is not a set path, as some fools and religious leaders spout with their pompous preaching. And now I must be off. I sense that I am needed elsewhere."

With that, the feeling of cold was gone. John slowly stretched out his hand into the darkness and felt nothing, nothing but the warm July air. He finally began to relax. That was certainly most enlightening. Was Death actually showing a spark of pity for his situation?

This was turning into a night to remember, and it was not quite half over. Curious about Death's gratuitous suggestion, John left the temporary safety of the Wills' doorway and walked unsteadily across the street past the Globe Inn to a small storefront.

But this was no ordinary business establishment. Strangely enough, the storefront window was completely covered from the inside with large swaths of black funeral bunting that had seen better days. This made it impossible to look inside. John thought it was odd that a merchant would deliberately hide the very products he was attempting to sell to the public.

A roughhewn wooden sign, absent of any paint or decorative scrollwork, hung loosely and slightly off kilter over the front door. It was obviously made in a rush to offer notification rather than to attract potential customers. The sign simply read:

DR. THOMAS BURNETTE

EMBALMING & SHIPPING

John had no idea what embalming meant, and although he was intrigued, he knew that night creatures' limitations prevented them from entering a building without expressed permission from someone inside it. Fortunately, there was a smaller sign nailed to the door frame that read:

HELP WANTED—INQUIRE WITHIN.

He certainly felt that this was serendipitous, or then again did his newly minted guardian angel, Death, have something to do with it? So many weird events were happening to him he was sure that absolutely nothing could surprise him this night.

Of course, he was dead wrong. John knocked sharply on the door three times and waited for a reply. It was not long in coming. A voice came from the rear of the store, followed by the sound of approaching footsteps. "Hold on a minute, please. I'll be right there; just got to wipe down a bit."

The footsteps grew louder until the doorknob jiggled as the door swung open. Standing there was a tall, thin, and tired looking man of about 40, wearing a smeared, discolored white apron fastened around his neck and waist.

Just what was smeared on that apron was anybody's guess. John was immediately hit with the sour smell of old blood, together with the odd scent of bitter almonds. His mouth instinctively began to water.

The two stood eyeing each other for several seconds before John broke the ice while pointing to the small sign. "Hello, I am here to inquire about work. Is a positon still available?"

The gentleman nearly jumped out of his shoes as his face beamed with excitement. He grabbed John's hand and pumped it vigorously while blurting out a rapid fire reply.

"Is it still AVAILABLE? Why, absolutely! Come in, DO come in. My name is Burnette, Doctor Thomas Burnette, embalming and shipping, at your service, sir. But you read the sign so you already know that, don't you?" John wondered when the man would come up for air, but he continued on just the same.

"Nine people have inquired about the position, and nine have turned it down. Can you believe it? Can you? You would think that I was asking them to rob graves, for Christ's sake. Ah, may I assume that you have no problems working with the dead? That reminds me, your hand is cold, sir. Are you well?"

"As well as can be expected," John replied blandly, "and to answer your question, no, I have no problems working with the dead. Exactly what are the particular requirements for employment?"

Burnette gave out a hearty laugh. "REQUIREMENTS! That's a good one, sir. Requirements, he asks! All right, let's seeeee...I'm afraid that a heartbeat is mandatory, and a strong stomach is preferred. As you might surmise, my standards are not particularly high at this point. I trust that you can fulfill at least one of those requirements?"

John's expression remained blank despite the fact that he was beginning to greatly appreciate the irony of his current situation. "I can most definitely fulfill at least one of your requirements, doctor; as to the other, well..."

Burnette interrupted; "We can only hope for the best concerning the strong stomach, can't we? After all, draining and re-filling corpses is not a run of the mill occupation, now is it?"

John was flabbergasted. "THAT'S what you do? THAT'S what this embalming thing is?"

Now Burnette was flabbergasted. "Why...yes, of course. Don't tell me you don't know about embalming. It became popular after my mentor, Thomas Holmes, prepared Colonel Ellsworth."

71

He waited for a spark of recollection on John's part but saw none, and resumed. "Ellsworth...Colonel Elmer Ellsworth...you know...the first martyr for the Union...killed in Virginia pulling down a Rebel flag...personal friend of President Lincoln...Where have you BEEN for the past several years?"

John quickly changed the subject. "I am willing to begin this very minute if that is acceptable to you, sir." His stomach began to growl noticeably. "I can only surmise that since it is nearly midnight and you are still hard at work that you have been hampered by a lack of assistance."

Burnette scoffed. "Assistance; I haven't had ANY assistance! That settles it; you're hired."

He ushered John inside and handed him an apron before he could think of anything else to ask. "The pay is a dollar a day. I will pay you half wages for the rest of the night. I just started a procedure when you knocked on the door. This body is slated for transport to Yonkers, New York in the morning, and I MUST have it ready."

John glanced over the doctor's shoulder to the center of the room. There he saw a corpse lying flat on barn boards suspended about three and a half feet in the air by molasses barrels on both ends. A pillow case was draped over the groin area, while the arms were stiff at the sides of the body. The eyes were closed, as was the mouth, but there was a thumb sized mark just above the navel.

It was innocent looking enough, but grim evidence of a sharpshooter's mini ball. Burnette continued. "This private lingered for several days at the hospital set up at the Lutheran Theological Seminary. It's quite a place. Is this your first corpse close up, Mr....I'm sorry, I never asked your name! My apologies."

"And I never gave it, sir. John Pike's the name, and no, this is not my first corpse. I spent some time down South before the war and witnessed...depravities performed on some unfortunate slaves. What exactly do you require me to do right now?"

"I was nearly finished washing this body. You may complete that task while I ready the equipment." Burnette handed a sponge and a bowl of soapy water to John, and then exited to a back room. He returned a few minutes later with a wooden bucket, two metal hand pumps with tubing, and a glass five gallon jug filled with a grayish liquid. In that short time John had nearly finished his task.

The doctor positioned his equipment on a small table and moved it close to the body. "Now we shall see about that strong stomach of yours, John."

He pulled a scalpel from a pocket in his apron and bent over the corpse, making quick incisions in the carotid artery and another in a nearby vein, then inserted the tubes from each pump into them. Pulling up on the handle of the second pump, he began to drain the blood from the body into the pump, which then exited the bottom of the pump via another tube into a bucket.

John used all of his willpower to remain calm as the blood began filling into the bucket. Each stroke of the pump made him more and more ravenous until he reached the point where he felt he was losing control. But the next moment, the doctor stopped, removed the tube, and sewed the cut in the vein.

He looked up at John; "How you doing so far, my friend? You look a bit pale."

"No problem doctor. I'm fine, thank you. What's the next step?"

"Well, now I'll begin to pump about two to three gallons of arsenic solution into the carotid artery, and we're on our way. That will help to preserve the body, hopefully until it arrives at its destination."

John was trying to think of anything he could to forget about the sweet bucket of blood just a few feet away. He closed his eyes, but the smell was intoxicating nevertheless. He tried some small talk. "Exactly how much do you charge for this type of procedure, doctor?"

"The going price is $25 dollars for an enlisted man and $50 dollars for an officer. Of course, shipping is extra, and that price is dependent on the length and mode of travel. Fortunately, Hanover Junction is not more than an hour or so away by wagon; transport from there by railroad will certainly help insure the body will remain intact on the journey.

Speed is of the essence. You just can't depend on ice to do the trick. It's far too problematic, particularly in these summer months. And don't forget, these men are from locales located all around the country."

John opened his eyes in surprise. "Tell me, why is the price DOUBLE for an officer? Do you perform any additional work?"

Burnette gave him an odd glance, and then looked away. 'Why...no...to be perfectly frank, the relatives of officers are usually more well to do, so...I can...charge more." He then became defensive and uneasy.

"I am only going by the rates first set by the good Dr. Holmes. Why don't you take that bucket of blood out back and dump it while I start refilling the carotid artery, and try not to spill it on the way. Blood can be very slippery after it hits the floor. I don't need you to break a leg right after I've hired you. By the bye, you don't have a problem with that task, do you?"

John smiled from ear to ear. "No problem at all, sir. I'll get right on it." He eagerly picked up the bucket by its rope handle and slowly headed out the back with careful half steps so as not to splash a single drop.

Once outside, he closed the door, looked around to make sure that he was alone, then raised the bucket to his lips and drank deeply until the bucket was completely drained. The heady liquid brought back his strength with each passing gulp.

Now there was no need to suffer the good doctor's company any longer.

Death had certainly hit the center of the bull's eye with the suggestion about visiting this establishment, and John was actually grateful, although confused. Just what was Death up to? He was not a being to be trusted, or was he?

There was nothing more to accomplish this night, and it was becoming clear that he had begun to overstay his welcome in Gettysburg. He had all the information he really needed, but more importantly, that Dhampir was on the way.

John thought it might be in his best interest to make himself scarce. After all, Death seemed quite pleased in pointing out that Lady Luck had soured on him; and why the constant references to the Vampire Council? Were there events developing at this very moment that Death was aware of but was unable, or rather unwilling, to reveal to him?

CHAPTER 8

Arrival Of The Dhampir

"I'm sorry to interrupt, but I must say, Cassidy, you have done outstanding work in getting this station back in operation. Knowing the reputation of White's Comanches as I do, I am certain that it was a monumental task. They are quite adept at destruction once they put their minds to it. Please go on." The Union officer leaned forward in his chair and listened with great interest.

"I thank you, Colonel Nagle. This place was a sorry lookin' mess, no doubt about it. Anyways, once we got word that our militia got whipped along the Susquehanna on the 26th, we sort of figured we wuz in for a visit. You don't have to be a bleedin' general to figure out that this rail junction was a prize heifer for them Rebs."

Nagle nodded in agreement. "Well, by God, we sure didn't have long to wait, cause the next day, we hear a lotta yellin' n' screamin' in the distance like the devil hisself was a comin' with the rest o' the fallen angels. In no time flat, a band of cavalry rides in and spreads out around the depot here and the hotel across the way.

I stepped out the front door to get a better look, and good Lord Almighty, there smack dab in front of me was this Reb officer on horseback, starin' up at the Hanover Station sign nailed to the overhang of the porch roof."

Nagle smiled. "I am sure that was Lt. Col. White. What did he do then, Cassidy?

"DO! Why, that sunofabitch sorta smiled liked your doin' now and waves to his men to go inside the building. That's when all hell broke loose. Those good ol' boys was havin' a real sweet time, choppin' things up while some others Rebs climbed up on the poles like raccoons an' cut the telegraph wires."

Cassidy shook his head in disgust. "They did some hollarin' and tore up a heap of equipment here inside, but the batteries for the telegraph are under the floorboards, so they didn't get them, an' I hid a telegraph key when I heard them ridin' in. They didn't stay for very long, but before they left, they burned our railroad turn table out back and the repairs barn too."

Nagle turned sympathetic in his tone. "That certainly was a harrowing experience for you sir. One threatening move could have cost you your life. These confederates are in enemy territory, and as such are not prone to give anyone the benefit of the doubt, soldier or civilian."

"I damn near wet my pants; that was the only threatening move I made once THEY showed up! I did feel kinda bad for Mr. Snyder…he's the station master…an' his wife an' kids. They stayed holed up scared to death on their side of the building where they live. The Rebs didn't bother them much, though. They rode off soon enough towards Gettysburg…to join the rest of Lee's army, I suppose."

Cassidy took a breath and finished up. "It really didn't take us very long to get the telegraph back up to snuff once the wires got re-strung. Say, colonel, you've come from Gettysburg. Were you there for the fightin'?"

Nagle became slightly defensive. "No…I'm afraid we missed the battle. My troops are here to hunt down…a very dangerous adversary."

"You mean like a spy or somethin' colonel?"

"Ah, yes, something like that. He was in Gettysburg during the fighting and beyond; now we are on his trail to make sure that...he can do no more damage."

Cassidy gushed. "Maybe I can help. Do you know what he looks like? Lots of people pass through this way, ya know."

"Why, you might be able to help at that. Do you know a young man by the name of John Larson?"

"Let's see. Larson...Larson...There are some Larson's in York; that's about 10 miles from here. I seem to recollect that they had a son, but that can't be the feller you're lookin' for. He died a few years back. It must be another Larson from hereabouts. You been to York yet, colonel?"

"No, I have been searching this general vicinity with a few trusted men. The rest of my troop has been concentrating on various parts within York proper. A location with a fair sized population would be more enticing to a fugitive with his... particular talents." The colonel opened his pocket watch and checked the time; it was almost noon.

"Mr. Cassidy, I have chosen this depot as a meeting place of sorts. Those who shall be arriving shortly will be very important to my investigation, and the utmost secrecy is necessary towards success. Would you mind if one of my men took you over to the hotel for lunch so I can speak with these people privately?"

Cassidy perked up. "Does that mean you're payin' TOO, colonel?"

Nagle sighed. "Yeesss, that means I'm paying too."

"WELL ALL RIGHT THEN! Let's get a goin'...Hey, wait a minute. I can't leave the station. What about the telegraph? There'll be no one here to take any messages, and there's a war on, ya know."

"Fortunately, I too happen to know code, Mr. Cassidy. It was part of my training. If anything does happen to come through over the wire while you're gone, I'll be sure to write it down. Now, do we have a deal?"

Cassidy made a puckered face like he was having trouble in an outhouse. Thinking was not his strong point. "Well, seein' as how you'll take any messages…yup, it's a deal. Just let me tell Mr. Snyder and we can be on our way. He's out front waitin' on the train a comin' in directly. It'll only take a minute."

Nagle sat stone-faced as Cassidy rushed out to the depot platform. Spectators would more than likely be a hindrance during the upcoming interrogation. A guard was quietly placed at the door linking the Snyder's residence to the telegraph and depot office. Once Cassidy was eagerly on the way to his free meal, the stage was set to Nagle's desire. He did not have long to wait.

A canvas covered army wagon pulled by a half dozen mules while being driven on by a Union soldier slowly sidled up to the depot. The driver quickly looked around, and satisfied that the station was empty for the moment except for the station master, gave out a low signal whistle.

Two armed soldiers jumped out the back of the wagon, followed by an indignant man and woman. The civilians were then dragged into the telegraph station. The colonel was pleased that the proceedings went off without incident.

The man glared at the colonel with rising anger, while the woman's eyes betrayed bewilderment. The officer was the first to break the silence. "Mr. and Mrs. Larson, I am Colonel John Nagle. I must first apologize for the manner in which you were…conveyed…to this meeting, but it is of the utmost importance that we meet face to face. Unfortunately…"

The husband exploded. "Just who the hell do you think you are? There are laws in this country against abduction. My wife and I have done nothing wrong, and we are staunch

Unionists. I am a lawyer sir, and since Pennsylvania is not
under martial law, what you have done is unwarranted and illegal. I DEMAND some answers. What is the name of your commanding officer?"

The colonel remained calm, almost to the point of disin-
terest. "You are in a position to demand nothing, Mr. Larson. It
is I who will demand some answers; as to illegal, we can bandy
that point back and forth. But legal or not, rest assured that the
importance of this meeting goes far beyond the laws of man."

Larson was undeterred. "What exactly are you a colonel of?
I see nothing on your uniform to designate you as belonging to
the infantry, cavalry...or artillery for that matter. That is highly
irregular, sir."

"You are very observant, and you are also absolutely correct. My position IS highly...irregular, but rest assured that we,
that is, my comrades and I, have tacit approval from the highest
military authority to conduct business as we see fit. Now, to MY
questions, and I hope that you will be cooperative, at least for
your wife's sake."

The woman grabbed her husband by the arm and pleaded
with him. "Oh, Hugh, let us find out what it is they want to
know and then they will let us go, is that not right, colonel?
After all, we are all on the same side, are we not?"

"Absolutely, Mrs. Larson; you have my word as a gentleman. I regret having to resort to such methods, but the stakes
are high. Now, let's get right down to it, shall we? Have either
of you seen or been in touch with your son John within the last
several weeks?"

Cory Larson's mouth opened wide and her eyes fluttered
back in her head as she fainted into her husband's arms. "You
filthy bastard," he cried, "My son is dead...drowned in
Louisiana and buried in the York cemetery these two years now.
What could possibly possess you to ask such a question?"

Nagle nodded as a train screeched into the station. "Yeeesss… possession…you hit the nail right on the head. I will ask you again, sir, have you seen or been in touch with your son within the last several weeks?"

"You are stark raving MAD! I refuse to participate in any of this foolishness. Neither my wife nor I will answer any of your questions, do you hear? Not a blessed one!"

Footsteps could be heard on the station platform as Cory Larson regained consciousness and began to speak with a weak but ominous tone. "I cannot believe that a Union officer could be so callous. I shall personally notify my friend Governor Curtin about this entire incident. It shall not go unpunished, I assure you."

Nagle patiently allowed her to finish her threat. "And madam, I assure you that you WILL answer ALL of my questions one way or another. I will only implore you this one time; better to speak with me now than my…associate." With that, a child's scream could be heard from the station master's residence.

"Mommy, mommy, I saw something horrible. It's coming this way. Don't let it in, please!"

A frightened woman soon responded to the plea. "Susan, get away from the window. It will see you. George! George! Dear God, where is my husband?"

All eyes focused on the telegraph station door as the sounds of slow, heavy foots on the station platform got louder and louder, and soon stopped. The door opened; two of Nagle's men armed with Sharps rifles entered the room. They appeared to be extremely uncomfortable as they nodded some secret affirmation to him, then stepped to either side of the door as another figure came into sight from around the corner.

There was a collective gasp from everyone in the room as a man entered flashing a wide smile; but this was no ordinary smile. The face was missing any semblance of lips or cheeks, producing the widest spread of gleaming white teeth in the most horrific nightmare imaginable.

As if that were not bad enough, the man's eyes were large, dull, coal black ovals that no one could to look into without an uncontrollable shiver; no pupil, no iris...nothing at all, just blackness totally devoid of emotion, and compassion.

Two more armed Union soldiers followed close behind him but stayed posted outside the door to the telegraph room. The colonel was aware that the stage had been set to his specifications, yet he appeared hesitant, almost afraid of what he had just orchestrated. The officer took a step backward as Hugh Larson put a protective arm around his wife's shoulder and then instinctively sidestepped in front of her.

So THIS was a Dhampir, Nagle thought to himself as he lowered his head slightly in shame. But it was too late to turn back now; much time and effort had been expended locating this...tool for the greater good. The silence was broken by the grinning thing, which scanned the room back and forth before it settled on the colonel.

"You have summoned me to track down and dispatch a vampire. I desire to start this hunt at once. What are your orders?" The voice had a sound like that of a screeching owl, but much more powerful.

"We have been searching for some time now," Nagle answered. Our network has relayed information that the one we seek is in this general area. We have come close several times, but success still eludes us. There is a possibility that the final piece of the puzzle may possibly rest with these two, who are its parents.

My men attempted to question them at their residence in York, but they were... uncooperative, to say the least. So now I turn this part of the investigation over to you so we may obtain the truth."

Hugh Larson was astounded. "My God, I was right; you ARE mad. Vampires exist only in legends and bedtime stories meant to keep frightened children from straying too far from the house at night. And how are WE are supposed to be its parents? You have…"

The Dhampir interrupted brusquely. "So these are the ones I am to question; fine then. Bring them…closer to me…that I may discover where their true loyalties lie.

The two guards nudged Hugh Larson forward with their rifle butts until he was a mere arm's length from the Dhampir. With a sharp, sweeping motion, it grabbed the startled man loosely by the throat and pulled him close enough for him to gag on its foul breath. Hugh was otherwise paralyzed with fear as he stared into the black eyes of the Dhampir.

The two stood together silently for several seconds, then the Dhampir released him. Hugh staggered backwards into the arms of his wife, who cradled him gently while she sobbed into his shoulder. "Whatever he told your men is the truth; this fool knows nothing of the vampire's whereabouts. Now, as to the bitch…"

Hugh flailed uselessly in an attempt to protect his wife, but the Dhampir nimbly grabbed him by his shirt collar and tossed him like a rag doll into a corner of the room, where he fell to the floor unconscious. The black eyes then turned their attention to Cory Larson, who whimpered as she dropped to her knees.

"Almighty God, protect me from this pestilence; but if it is your will that I now depart from this world, save my soul that I may enjoy everlasting life."

She barely got the words out when the Dhampir grabbed her by the hair and jerked her face up into his shadowy gaze as he spoke. "I don't like that kind of talk. It makes me feel unwanted."

After a long moment of silence, the Dhampir gnashed its teeth and flung her limp body to the floor. "She too is of no use to us. Take them away."

Nagle piped up. "Vampires have the power to hypnotize their subjects without their having the slightest knowledge of it. Are you sure that they have not been conditioned to lie under just this type of circumstance?

The Dhampir let out a shrill, high pitched laugh that chilled the soldiers to the bone. The sentries gripped their rifles tightly and held them close to their breasts. "I am not any circumstance, Freemason. There is no one who can hide their thoughts from ME. It is one of my special…gifts, shall we say?"

Nagle acquiesced. "All right, so they have no knowledge of their son's whereabouts. What is to stop them from reporting what has just taken place to the local authorities? We do not have the time to be sidetracked by such trivialities."

The Dhampir sounded annoyed as he swatted his hand in the air. "I have erased the episode from their feeble memories. They will remember nothing of the interrogation, who was there, or where it took place. Now, throw them back into the cart and take them home. They will awake in due time this evening. Their scum of a son is not in York, I can attest to that fact."

Nagle began to wring his hands slowly as he was still unconvinced. "Are you positively sure? I have been charged by the highest authority to destroy this thing. It is of the…"

In a flash the Dhampir was looming directly in front of the colonel, smiling once again. Its speed was astounding. "Would you be more convinced if I said that I would… swear to God? Or would you prefer…Supreme Being? I believe that is the favorite moniker of you particular organization?"

Nagle stepped back and took a deep breath. This association was not going to be a pleasant experience in any shape or form. "There is no need to be blasphemous; your word is good enough for me. Let us be gone from here... but where do we go next?"

The Dhampir gazed out the window. "To the last place he left his mark, that place you call...Gettysburg. I know that your men have already searched the town, but this is a cunning adversary despite his youth. He may still be in hiding, or he may have left just enough of a trail for me to follow. In either case, I will find him and send him to oblivion, the fitting place for his kind."

As the group made preparations to leave, the telegraph wire began to chatter. The colonel casually walked over to the key board, but made no attempt to decipher the tapping in the communication. He picked up a pen, dipped it in ink, and scribbled down a short message as a near promise to Cassidy. It read simply: *What hath God wrought?*

CHAPTER 9

Up Close And Personal

T he Rebel corporal greeted the approaching surgeon with hopeful skepticism. "Hallo there, Doctor O'Neal. Are you fixin' to clean up the wound or saw off my leg tonight? I been a keepin' still on this here straw bed like you said, an' I was even awavin' my hat to keep the flies from a lightin'. How'd I do?"

O'Neal bent down and carefully removed the bloody bandages that protected the soldier's ankle. Immediately a sickly sweet smell wafted up as he uncovered the hidden red and purple blotches around a dirty bullet hole. He sighed deeply as he looked into the anxious face of a middle aged man who was about to become an invalid, IF he was lucky.

'I'm very sorry, Fenton, but the leg's gone gangrene. It's got to come off or you'll be dead in...two days tops. I'll do my best to stay below the knee, but I really can't promise you anything.

Fortunately, we do have an ample supply of chloroform, so I can spare you the initial pain of the operation. After that, it will all depend on how your body reacts to this. We can't really tell in these cases. It's different from one man to the next."

The soldier sagged and laid his head back on a sack of meal, staring at the barn roof. "It's gotta come off, he says; he sounds like he's gonna take off a shirt or somethin'. And what

86

happens after that? I get packed off to some prisoner of war camp, and if I'm LUCKY, I can hobble on back to New Market after the war and do what on my farm? NOTHIN'...nothin' with but one good leg.

How'm I supposed to tend my farm and feed my family? My wife's a frail little thing and the boys are too young to be of any real use. Go on; tell me what I can do back there?"

The doctor closed his eyes. "I can't tell you, Fenton. All I can tell you is it still has to come off...after that, I just don't know."

"Well hurry up and saw it off then before I change my mind, and don't you forget to use some of that chloro...stuff you spoke about."

"All right then," O'Neal spoke calmly; "Let me get the stall ready." He moved to the center of the barn. "Orderly...you, McMillan, lend a hand here, along with...what's your name, son?"

"My name is John Pike, sir. I couldn't sleep and came by to see if I could be of any help."

"Well, you've come to the right place. You and McMillan grab a hold of Corporal Fenton there and lay him down in that stall in the corner. Be sure to scrounge up plenty of bandages too. I'll get my kits."

The two men put the silent, teary eyed soldier on a pine board and gently carried him over to the stall, resting him atop several blood soaked bales of hay. This place had been used for operations before. The doctor returned with two innocent looking leather covered boxes and placed them on the stall shelf. The first one was chock full of small glass bottles of various shapes and colors. O'Neal fingered his way through them carefully until he found the one he wanted and lifted it out. The stained and peeling label read:

CHLOROFROMIUM

T. Morris Perot & Co.

"This is the little beauty for you, corporal. A few whiffs of this liquid and I guarantee you will feel no pain whatsoever. You have my word as a gentleman."

Fenton was visibly touched. "Your word is good enough, doctor. You've looked after me just like I was a true blue Yankee, and that's a fact. Well... let's get this shebang a goin' sawbones."

John watched O'Neal open the second case; its contents were of a more foreboding nature, and included all manner of saws, scalpels, forceps, and scissors, amongst other things he knew not. The nickname Fenton threw offhandedly at his doctor was indeed going to be quite accurate.

Fortunately, the instruments were out of the prostrate soldier's line of sight, and would not add to his tension, which was already severe but controlled.

John weighed his own thoughts and reasoned that what this Rebel was experiencing at this very moment was even more terrifying than a bayonet charge; at least in a charge you were alongside your comrades, and could hold onto the possibility of coming through the engagement unscathed, however slim that might be. Right now, Fenton was certain of having a limb hacked off his body, and there was nothing in this world he could do about it.

O'Neal put on an apron previously stained with dried blood and prepared to operate. "McMillan, I want you to administer the..."

"Excuse me, doctor," the orderly interrupted in a pleading tone, "I just can't stomach any more of this right now. Please let me get someone to take my place."

The doctor was irritated, but understood and restrained himself. "Go ahead then, but be quick about it. You, John, I want you to cut off the lower half of Fenton's pants leg to just above the knee; you got that?"

"Yes, sir," John responded obediently. As he went about his task, he felt a cold shiver go up his back. Glancing up, he saw McMillan's replacement, and suddenly, a future was not in the cards for Corporal Fenton. Death itself was attending this operation, and yet provided some reassuring words.

"I have assisted in a number of these procedures, doctor."

"But have you ever administered chloroform?"

"Oh, yes, sir, I have been schooled in the proper technique."

"Fine; douse a rag and give the corporal a dose. The sooner he's unconscious, the better off he'll be."

Death opened the bottle of chloroform and spread some lightly on a bandage, and then quickly corked the bottle. John looked down at Fenton, whose eyes were like slits, as though he did not want to witness the proceedings. The rag was placed under his nose, and his eyes opened wide as he stiffened with his first whiff of the potent mixture.

O'Neal spoke serenely; "Take, long, slow breaths, Fenton. Think about being home with your family, sitting on that front porch. It will help to calm you down." The soldier had his arms at his side, gripping the edges of the board, but soon his eyes fluttered, and his hands went limp. Death could be heard counting to a low 10, and then removed the rag.

"Nice job, orderly. You HAVE done this procedure. Why haven't I seen your face before?" John perked up; he was interested in what the reply might be.

"I have assisted in a good number of the hospitals, doctor, but mostly in the town. This is my first time out on the Mummasburg Road and Mr. Schriver's farm."

"I see; well, keep up the intermittent counts with the chloroform. John, hold the leg down straight and keep it firmly in place while I begin. I don't want any involuntary movement." O'Neal started by applying a tourniquet above the infection to stop the flow of blood to the ankle; then he carefully cut through the skin with a small scalpel and flapped it up and over the wound.

John was impressed with the doctor's skill. He glanced at Death, who faithfully stood over Fenton and continued to administer the chloroform as directed without any outward show of emotion. O'Neal sighed with resignation as the real work began, partly because it signified defeat, and partly because of the utter finality of the act itself.

He went back to his kit and took out what looked remarkably like a common hacksaw and started his see saw motion back and forth until he had severed the limb completely. The final cut made a dull scrape as it hit the board Fenton was lying on. O'Neal picked up the ankle, looked at it with a face of resignation, and flung it into the corner of the stall.

He stopped for a moment. "Not much of a thank you to a soldier for service to his country, even if he is on the wrong side." But there was no time for further reflection; time was of the essence. The final step was the delicate sewing of the major veins and arteries, followed by a bandage wrap.

Fifteen minutes had gone by, minutes that felt would have felt like days to Fenton except for the precious chloroform. O'Neal wiped the saw and scalpel dry on his dirty apron and returned them to their places in the kit. "Thank you boys, you were a great help to me.

He can be returned to his place in the barn; just check on the bandages in an hour. There may be some minor weeping, but I don't expect any excess loss of blood. If there is, call me. I'll be in my tent by the house. I've GOT to get some sleep…been up for 24 hours straight."

90

O'Neal picked up his cases and trudged out into the night. If John had learned anything from this final reconnaissance, it was that he believed this civil war would go down in history like no other. He even went as far as to envision no executions of military leaders upon its conclusion. There was just too much humanity on display.

This Second American Revolution, as the Rebels reveled in naming it, appeared to generate carnage during an actual battle, but once a man was wounded, it was almost as though a candle was blown out and the hatred ceased, at least for many of the actual participants.

Now if only that feeling could be somehow transferred to the rabid politicians on both sides fueling this war, could all be well again, with compromise and clear heads?

"Never happen," John grunted to himself. Humans were the real abominations, not his kind. They killed for pleasure or gain; night creatures did so for survival. Where was the justice in the sanctimonious Freemasons and their Dhampir lap dog tracking him down?

Death was able to read his thoughts and broke John's reverie. "Justice is a man-made habit, my dear Mr. Larson, and as such, can be molded to whatever shape or form suits…the victors. You do not see it in the natural world, yet animals do quite well without it. I told you the other night to leave Gettysburg, and you are still here. I must chalk that up to stupidity and stubbornness…perhaps both!"

"You've found a sweet killing zone here for yourself," John retorted. "This is like shooting fish in a barrel going from house to barn and church, picking out who's to live and who's to die. What are you going to do with Corporal Fenton?"

"He will pass away in the morning, and I will be at his side to comfort and guide another life force into the light. I told you once before that my motives have been misunderstood throughout history. Only the wise see me for what I truly am, a constant companion on the journey of life, waiting patiently for the moment to reward those who have made the honest effort."

Death then shot John a knowing glance. "But enough of this; the Dhampir has ARRIVED, and YOUR time is up. You must excuse me now. There is a lost soldier lying in the woods who requires my presence. I will see to it that he does not die alone in the darkness."

John watched as Death turned abruptly and walked out of the barn turned military hospital. There were hundreds of casualties at this location alone, and thousands in the general vicinity of Gettysburg. He wondered how his sometime associate and tormentor could accomplish his mission.

"Mission," John murmured; it was time to get back to his, especially if what Death said about the Dhampir was true. He slipped out of the barn and found a secluded spot free from the flotsam and jetsam that make up a military hospital. A quick thrust and he was above the tree line and into the night sky, with a notion to head on the Cashtown Pike to Lee's army.

But the flight was short lived. He noticed the flicker of torches moving slowly in the darkness and decided on a final investigation. The search for missing soldiers by comrades on a battlefield at night was common enough, but it had been over 10 days since the lead had stopped flying.

Who was out and about near midnight, and why? The Freemasons would not be looking for any of John's sanctuaries during the evening hours; that didn't make any sense. No, this was something else, so he drifted along until he caught up to the torches at a small clearing and touched down into the canopy of an outlying tree.

A closer inspection revealed it was a burial party of four men; three Confederates and one Union guard. The lead Rebel was carrying a torch and several long handled shovels, followed closely behind by two raggedly dressed fellow soldiers with a makeshift litter made of fence rails and a sagging canvas.

A Union guard brought up the rear of the macabre procession with a torch in one hand and a rifle slung over his other shoulder. Despite being outnumbered and alone, he did not appear nervous. The prisoners chosen were all used up, and barely up to the task of a burial detail.

The guard spoke first with an almost reverential tone. Although he was burying an enemy, there was no cause to be vengeful. "All right boys, this is good enough; set em' down right here and start to diggin'."

The two litter bearers happily complied with the order and lowered the litter to the ground. It revealed a blackened, bloated body of a fellow Confederate who by the looks of it had been forgotten in the woods and had half of his head blown away.

While avoiding a direct gaze on the body was fairly simple, one of the Rebels could stand the smell no more and began to vomit profusely. The other two did not wait for him to stop and grabbed the shovels to begin digging the grave.

John found this interesting. When the hole was nearing three feet deep, two of the men went back over and picked up the litter, but the canvas ripped in half and unceremoniously dropped the stiffened body to the ground again.

John was curious as to how they would now get the corpse into the adjacent grave without soiling themselves, but the practical aspect of war was on display. They took hold of their fence posts, then poked and rolled the body until it landed perfectly in the hole. Fortunately, they did not miscalculate on the length of the grave; that would have made for some unappetizing decisions.

The stained, foul smelling canvas was carefully removed from the rail poles and placed over the body. Although unknown, at least this soldier would have a burial shroud. He was one of the lucky ones in that regard.

The two Rebels grabbed their shovels and took turns flinging dirt until only a slight mound remained to pat down. All four men stepped back and stared at it for a moment.

The Union guard spoke up softly. "Does anyone…want to say a prayer over this…poor bastard…before we go back?" The rest said nothing at first; they just continued to stare at that innocent looking mound of earth, knowing full well that rotting corpse could have been any of them. Finally, one stepped forward and cleared his throat to speak as they all took off their hats.

"Lord grant that this Southern soldier reaches the gates o' heaven for givin' up his life for his country. God bless him, and God bless Robert E. Lee… I sure hope St. Peter ain't no Yankee." With muffled chuckles and a solemn amen, the four turned around quietly and made their way back towards the hospital area.

John wondered what the dead soldier's family was doing at this very moment; were they sleeping soundly after an early evening prayer to the Almighty to keep watch over their father and husband until he came home to them safe and sound? Yes, John decided; he was sure of it.

CHAPTER 10

Capture, Trial, And Punishment

E ven in mid-flight, it wasn't difficult for John to pick up the trail of Lee's army so late in the game. All he had to do was follow the smell of the blood.

The Chambersburg Pike had been pock marked with the crimson liquid that had seeped out of the hospital wagons during their tortuous journey home to the safety in Virginia. Even though it had rained heavily and the wagons had set out more than 10 days ago, the scent was STILL there for him to pick up.

He slowly passed over the very hotel where he had initiated his attacks on the Confederates at the end of June, and continued beyond Cashtown through the South Mountain Pass. He veered south at Greenwood, and continued through Duffield, New Franklin, and Marion.

Along the way he continually saw the remnants of this hideous retreat: cracked wagon wheels, broken axles, crates, and a number of mules that had been shot due as a result of breaking their ankles along the muddy terrain.

The road was nearly empty at this late hour, but he spied a lone covered wagon wending its way toward Greencastle and decided to hitch a ride and rest for a bit at the same time. He touched down lightly onto the canvas roof near the front bow and lay face down.

A quick peek over the edge revealed a father and his son of about 14 years of age driving the mule team along. The boy was peppering his dad with questions.

"Do you think the Rebs are gonna make it back to Virginia, pa?"

"Can't say for sure, son; it's hard to believe they'll ALL get to cross over the Potomac. Your Uncle Eli was watching them as they passed his place. He said the wagon train was spread out for nearly 15 miles."

"That's not good, is it, pa?"

"No, son; the more stretched out the column, the more vulnerable it is to attack. The Union cavalry has been harassing them ever since they snuck out of Gettysburg in that God awful rainstorm on the 4th of July. It's been hell to pay for them ever since."

"Do we know where the Rebs are now, pa?"

"I heard tell they're still movin' southwest and lookin' to cross over the Mason Dixon Line into Maryland."

"Is that good for them?"

"I think so, son; I hate to say it, but there are lots of Southern sympathizers in Maryland, and that's for certain. I heard tell there were Unionist townsfolk along the way doin' their best to gum up the works by breaking their wagon spokes n' such. Don't know how true that is, though. If they were to get caught in the act, the Rebs would probably be within their rights to shoot em'."

"But what about our troops, pa? Why ain't they bustin' out after em'? We won, didn't we? It was the Rebs who snuck out when no one was lookin'."

"I don't know what's goin' on in Gettysburg right now, son; could be the army's all fought out. It happens. I'm sure General Meade knows what he's doin'. Maybe that's why he only has his cavalry nippin' at their heels."

"You like General Meade, don't you, pa?"

The man laughed. "You mean the goggle eyed old snapping turtle? Yes, son, I surely do. I was with him at Glendale when he got wounded real bad."

"Worse than you, pa?"

"Yes, son, worse than me, but I was the one who got sent home for good when my foot got blown off by that goddamned artillery shell...excuse my cussin'. I promised your ma I would try to stop that, but it's hard when you've been in the army; seems like all the boys ever did there was cuss, and cuss up quite a storm, too."

"You'd still be in the army if that hadn't happened, wouldn't you, pa? I heard you tell Uncle Eli you liked fightin' for the Union."

"Yes, son, I woulda stayed, but I coulda been long dead by now, too...so in a way, losin' my foot got me back to you an' your mother for good. Many of my friends are never gonna' come home to their families."

"Where do ya think the Rebs are gonna try to cross over, pa?"

"Well, my guess is they may try for Williamsport or Falling Waters. There are some decent fords around for the wagons to use. Everything depends on the river, son. If its' swollen, all hell will break loose when the cavalry catches up to them.

But it won't be easy for us, and that's for damned...darned sure. They got a good man in that General Imboden. Eli heard from a Reb prisoner captured by our troopers that he's the one in charge of that there wagon train, and he was chosen by General Lee himself."

John's ear's picked up. This was a golden piece of information! If he could catch up with the wagon train and find an opportunity to disable this General Imboden like he did the others at Gettysburg, there was a chance that the pursuing Union cavalry could bag a good many of the wagons and wounded. Wagons and mules were becoming a precious commodity in the South, nearly as precious as men.

Perhaps Death was wrong in assuming that Lady Luck had deserted him. John smiled at the thought of it, but as it turned out, that would be his last smile for a good many years.

As the wagon approached a massive maple tree, he thought he detected glints of amber coming from the limbs hanging up and over the road, but he paid it no mind. The wagon passed slowly under the darkened green canopy, and at that very moment he felt a powerful claw on the back of his neck.

The wagon continued on its solitary way, but John suddenly found himself hanging in mid-air. Before he even had the chance to look up a sack was thrown over his head and cinched shut; then he felt himself catapulted into the night sky.

As he began to flail about wildly in fear, his hands and legs were grabbed and held fast in vice like grips that made him howl in pain. Whatever had hold of him was far stronger than anything he had ever encountered, including his old master, Jacques Dumaine.

His thoughts shot back to his friendly enemy, Death. He was warned repeatedly that the Dhampir was closing in on him. Now John feared he would have to pay the ultimate price for his insolence.

"Well, come on, why don't you get this over with? End me and be done with it," he roared in a mixture of defiance and desperation. There was no reply, only the soft sound of the night breeze and a flapping of wings as he instinctively felt himself moving east.

He stopped struggling altogether; there was no point. This Dhampir possessed unimagined strength. It then occurred to John that his captor could be returning him to Gettysburg so he could be dispatched at the hands of the Freemasons.

How pleased they would be. He could see it all now. The hypocritical bastards would be chanting and performing some mumbo jumbo rituals, dressed in robes and invoking God's name as they sanctimoniously slaughtered him.

Despite his temporary lack of sight, he knew that they were moving to the east. Yes, he was going back all right. As they grew nearer to Gettysburg, he caught the slightest smell of blood and decay. Sanitation had improved markedly since the Rebels left the town, but he could not help but detect an odd, musty odor around him since his capture. Was this the Dhampir's scent?

John never got the chance to answer his own question. They went into a steep dive, and then suddenly, he was flung downward until he hit the ground and crashed into unconsciousness. He had no idea how long he was knocked out. It could have been several minutes or several hours. There was no way of telling, not that it mattered at this point.

He lay still until his head cleared, then he sat up and made a slow movement to remove the sack, half expecting to have his hand wacked or jerked back until his bones cracked. And yet nothing happened when he loosened the cinch and removed his cover.

What met his eyes was a sight that sent a wave of fear cascading over every part of his body. It was not the Dhampir and the Freemasons after all; that would have been mere child's play in comparison. No, this was something FAR more sinister.

He found himself in a circle of what he perceived were night creatures, but these beings were old, ancient in truth. That accounted for the musty smell he had detected. There were eight of them, and John could not have conceived of a more hideous sight in his wildest nightmare.

They appeared to be an equal measure of half human and half condor, with the legs and general shape of men, while their arms had morphed into stringy, grotesque, shredded wings, and long, gnarled talons in place of hands.

But the most revolting feature was their faces. Beady reddish amber eyes were set between long, hooked beaks, surrounded by wrinkled skin and spiked sprouts of hair.

A closer inspection revealed that each of them had, at one point in time, a distinct color, but the vibrant hues had long since faded over the centuries. Now, the colors were mere pale wisps of their former brilliance. This was the setting in which John would have his introduction to the Vampire Council.

John noticed Houck's Ridge not far off in the background. He WAS back on the battlefield after all, in an open, triangular field that held no possible avenue of escape.

He sighed and dejectedly cast his eyes to the ground in despair, then saw that he was dead center in the middle of a large, five pointed star of stones, with a circle of tree branches surrounding them all. It was at that moment that John was struck by the thought that his trial was about to begin.

They stood motionless around him like rigid oaks, with eyes so piercing John could not hold their gaze. Finally, the night creature of pale blue was the first to speak.

"John Larson, you have been summoned before this ancient Council to explain your actions. It has been charged that you have violated the most sacred rule of the night creature, NOT to interfere in the affairs of mankind. How do you plead, guilty or innocent?"

John gathered up what little bravado he had left. "You know who I am, but I do not know any of my accusers. That does not seem fair. Will this be a council of facts and reason, or is all of this a sham? Just who ARE you to accuse and put me on trial?"

The blue creature answered with controlled anger. "Your ignorance will be of little help to you, and your disrespect will be taken into account. WE are the fathers of our race, the first night creatures from around this world. Our age is measured in the thousands of years, AND...we are the guardians of man's history."

John was astounded. "Did I hear you correctly? Did you say MAN'S HISTORY?"

"Yes; we represent the first of our kind in each of the eight continents."

"You mean seven continents."

"I said EIGHT!" He pointed a bony talon in a circular motion at each of the respective night creatures. "Each of my brothers represents a continent and its history within its spectrum of light."

He singled them out one by one. "Africa...is black, North America...green, South America...scarlet, Europe...violet, Australia...teal, Asia...yellow, Antarctica...white." He halted for a moment; "And my own color represents a continent lost long, long ago. This august body is cognizant of all the world's secrets and mysteries."

There was a long pause. "How can I even begin to tell you of the knowledge we possess? We know who were the true builders of the pyramids...the meaning of the lines at Nasca...the hidden message of Stonehenge...the river that hides Mokele-Mbembe...the way through the Puerta de Haya Marca...the burial site of Alexander the Great."

The creature then bowed its head in sadness and gestured to its own light blue hew; "Even the location of my poor, doomed Atlantis. We know ALL of this…and much, much more."

John stiffened. "If you know all of that, then you know my reason for attacking the Rebel generals as I did, in order to save the United States. This country can become a beacon for all nations around the globe, and I cannot stand by and have it destroyed by fools and white slavers who are thinking only of money and their own self interests."

The blue creature raised his head and looked about with his hands in the air. "My brothers, he is condemned by his own words! There is not the slightest hint of regret or shame in his voice. Are there any here who will stand up for him?"

Only silence followed; "John Larson, you have taken it upon yourself to alter the course of man's history. What is done cannot be undone, but this council can make certain you do no MORE harm. Do you know where you are standing?"

"Why, yes; I'm…near Houck's ridge…on the battlefield."

"No, you fool; look closer. You have been placed inside the pentacle—a five pointed star within a circle. The points of the star represent earth, air, fire, water, and spirit. The circle represents the eternal cycle of life. THAT is to be your sentence; that is to be your fate."

John was shocked. "I don't understand. You're not…going to KILL me?"

The blue creature lowered its voice. "There are some things worse than death, and you will soon understand what that means."

A rectangular, brown glass quinine bottle was tossed into the circle. "Because you have altered the history of this nation, your sentence shall be the Noinjimo. This punishment has rarely been meted out due to its...severity, but you have left us no other alternative."

John began to shiver uncontrollably. He was never more frightened than at this very moment, not even when Dumaine was ripping at his throat back on the plantation. "And what is this...Noinjimo?" The answer was cryptic at first, but became more specific.

"It is the never ending circle, much like the pentacle you inhabit at this moment. Your body will be transformed into a mist, forced into this glass container, and buried. You will not die, you will not sleep, you will be fully conscious, and you will stay that way for all time.

In a thousand years or more, IF you are fortunate, you may go insane and find some small semblance of peace in your delirium, but you will ALWAYS be aware of your eternal confinement. THAT is the judgment of this council."

The night creatures began to step forward until they reached the pile of tree limbs surrounding the pentacle, all the while producing a low, guttural sound. Suddenly, the wooden circle burst into white flame, and all began a hypnotic, rhythmic chant: " Ginoosteeg Monteeju...Ginoosteeg Monteeju... Ginoosteeg Monteeju."

With each passing incantation, John felt himself becoming weak, dizzy, and disoriented; worse than that, he saw his hands disappearing before his very eyes. In another instant, before he could utter a single word of protest, his form was gone, and he felt as though he were being pulled through a long tunnel that grew darker and darker as he continued on.

Finally, his conscious mind coalesced, and he came to the realization that he was indeed inside the bottle; alive, rational, in full control of his mind and his memories, but in the grips of a dread beyond words, without a mouth or voice to release his terror.

The former medicinal bottle turned prison was corked tightly shut, smothered over with hot wax, and finally a dab of blood from the blue night creature's talon. This was a seal that could not be broken. There WAS no way out for him. He thought he could detect a distant voice call out; it was the green night creature.

"You shall be buried in a special place that shall remain undisturbed, in a place that is feared by many. It is an area known as the Devil's Den. I believe that you may be aware of this particular location. A great snake was once thought to inhabit the area among the surrounding boulders.

According to legend, it was seen infrequently, but more often than desired. The local farmers could never quite entice the snake from its deep, underground lair to kill the hated thing. It was at one time foolishly referred to as the devil himself.

You may be interested to know that it is still here, winding its way deep beneath the rocks and boulders to avoid the gaze of men. I daresay it will be your only neighbor. Now you have all the time in the world to ponder over your transgressions."

John somehow was aware that soil was being placed over the bottle and tamped down intermittently for a snug fit. All light and sound from the outside world was fading out. Nothing was being left to chance. He had been cast down deep into a black, silent, earthen hole…his new home for all eternity!

CHAPTER 11

The Great Escape

T hose first few weeks were by far the worst. John's mind spun in a continuous loop of unbridled hatred, abject terror, and total despair. His world was one of isolation and deprivation. The only things that remained were his thoughts and feelings.

He could not even count on the blessed oasis of sleep for a short respite, as he was in a perpetual state of self-awareness. This was the exquisite punishment handed down by the council, a hideous torture that had been meted out to only a chosen few night creatures that had disturbed the path of man's destiny.

However, in a few months, John actually felt the bottle grow perceptibly cooler. He reasoned this to be the onset of the harsh, Pennsylvania winter. He envisioned snow falling silently over his glass tomb and the rest of the expansive battlefield. The temperature fluctuations would be his way of keeping track of time; seasonal weather changes could be counted.

He wondered if this was a mistake on the part of the council, or another way for them to taunt John by allowing him to count the years as they passed by. There WAS the outside possibility that in its haste, the ancient night creatures had not buried him deep enough. Was this Death's whisper for him to keep faith in his eventual escape?

It was the lone hope available to John, and he clung to it gratefully, almost reverently. The seasons passed by in an agonizingly slow pace.

He kept hold on his sanity with the decision to carefully reflect on every moment his past life, from his first childhood memory all the way up through his imprisonment in exquisitely minute detail. This exercise kept his mind occupied through to the turn of a new century.

He often wondered what the year 1900 was like, from women's fashions to politics. After that, he often speculated about the outcome of the war, but soon came to the realization that his actions at Gettysburg had indeed been a lynchpin to an ultimate Union victory.

Why else would Death have taken such a keen interest in his particular situation? Why else would the Vampire Council have met to render such a harsh judgment against him?

Yes, he came to terms with himself that the North had won the war. It did provide him with some measure of solace, and if this was his reward, then so be it. But could the infant Republican Party find the right combination to win the peace?

He had faith in President Lincoln, whom he saw as a fair and decent man interested in ALL Americans. It was those Radical Republicans within the party that were of chief concern to John.

If they became too powerful and decided to go down a vengeful path of spite and retribution, the nation could very well be scarred for another 100 years. Southerners were a proud and stubborn lot, even in defeat.

They would not take kindly to what they perceived to be insults or ill treatment. He hoped old Abe could make good use of his homespun humor and status as a victorious Commander in Chief to keep the Radicals in check while he dutifully rebuilt a decimated South for the good of the nation.

John would count another 200 changes of the seasons pass by. The United States was at the halfway point of the 20th century. He continued to wonder what great technological marvels had been invented.

Before his imprisonment, he had witnessed firsthand what the rifled musket and the mini ball could do to an assaulting force, along with the breach loader and those new infernal machines. Military technology was far ahead of military tactics. He saw the effect of that on the eve of the 3rd day of the battle at Gettysburg.

Factories had also been churning out all manner of goods with their mechanical contraptions, and foundries had given birth to iron ships, signaling the death knell for wooden fleets all around the world.

The telegraph had greatly improved communications, and the steam engine enabled troops and civilians to travel in relative speed and safety. Anesthetics such as chloroform and ether brought blessed relief to the injured, while the camera thrust the bloody harvest of war into the hearts and minds of Americans everyday lives.

John believed that if man could only control his inner demons, the possibilities for advancement were endless. But what if man himself had not progressed? How many more wars would have been fought around the world while he lay trapped under the ground? Did the United States of America even exist?

Those were the tantalizing questions John bandied about over the final half of the 20th century. And while he pondered the future of his country, he thought he detected movement from the bottle, almost imperceptible at first, but more and more as the years passed.

He had no idea what had caused the shift, but it WAS happening. This began to give him some sliver of hope that his lot was somehow improving, but then the movement slowed to a near dead stop.

More precious years passed by; John ultimately lost interest and gave up keeping track of the seasons above him. He finally settled into a dull, morose lethargy that showed no sign of letting up. In the back of his mind, he knew that he was becoming unhinged.

The blue night creature's offhand comment came back to haunt him: "If you are fortunate, you may go insane and find some small semblance of peace in your jumbled thoughts."

And then something very strange happened. He suddenly heard the ground shake and rumble above him, then taper off to silence. At first, he thought that he had imagined it; after all, he WAS losing control of his faculties. There was no telling from here on in what fantasies his mind might conjure up.

The ground shook again, and again, until he actually felt the long dormant prison that held him give out a savage jerk, as though he were being hauled to the surface. Was he being dug up? Had the council decided that his punishment had been too harsh after all? No one else knew that he was buried here; it HAD to be them. He would be set free!

John's hope and excitement was unbounded as he waited for his deliverance. But nothing of the sort occurred. Above him, machines that he could never have dreamed of were being used throughout the Devil's Den and Houck's Ridge areas—trucks, chain saws, wood chippers, and stump grinders. Busy men wearing hard hats, overalls, and thick canvas gloves were methodically cutting down X marked trees and scrub shrubbery.

But the workers were not alone on the battlefield this cold, late winter's morning. Three women approached a pickup truck which had logos that read Danny Longo Tree Care on its front doors. They sidled up to the cab and attempted to speak with the man behind the wheel. "Are you in charge of this construction site?"

"That's right. I'm Danny...What can I do for you?"

A tall, thin, smarmy looking woman with large round glasses peered out from her spectacles with contempt. To Danny, she resembled a furious Olive Oyl from the old black and white Popeye cartoons.

"You must STOP this wanton destruction of the trees. They are living things! Where will the birds go to nest and rest? What happens if the soil begins to wash away? This is a park; it's supposed to have trees and grass, and you're ripping it all out and leaving a barren landscape. This is a sacrilege!"

Longo sighed and addressed her as tactfully as possible, although tact was not one of his strong suits. "Man, I wish the NPS guys were here. Lady, I remember you from the meeting last month. I'll tell you now what I told you then, not that you'll listen now either. My company has been LEGALLY contracted by the National Park Service to remove selected trees and vegetation as part of Gettysburg's Master Plan to return the battlefield to its 1863 appearance."

The woman squealed. "But this is a National PARK! You can't do this! We'll sue you and take every penny and piece of equipment that you've got. I'm going back to contact the Audubon Society, the Arbor Day Foundation...and the American Civil Liberties Union. Trees have rights too!"

"Lady, if you really want to sue someone, then sue the guy who sold you those glasses. Look, this is a MILITARY park, and the people who come here should be given the chance to see and understand how and why things happened like they did during the battle. It seems pretty reasonable and straight forward to me, and I'm not a history guy."

The trio stormed off with a warning message from the leader, who waved a bony index finger back at him. "You think you're so smart. This isn't the end of it, not by a long shot. I'll get a judge to grant me a court injunction to halt this destruction; that's when I'll sleep easy."

Longo had suffered enough, and he shouted out a reply just as they were about to move out of earshot. "Lady, if you sleep easy, it'll be all by yourself." Then he turned to address his crew, who had stopped work and were watching the proceedings with great interest, as there's nothing quite like watching the boss on the spot, getting HIS balls broken for a change.

"God, what a miserable bitch," he said in disgust as his face puckered up. "Could you ever imagine being MARRIED to that? I wouldn't touch her wearing a body condom." The crew guffawed and nodded their heads in agreement, then resumed working as though the altercation had never happened.

But something HAD happened. As one of the larger trees roots were being ripped out of the ground, it pushed the quinine bottle against a rock as it was being drawn closer to the surface. John could sense a difference.

There was a minute crack in the glass, but more importantly, the bottle was no longer below the frost line. All he had to do now was wait; that was something he had been doing for 142 years.

Nothing of note transpired for the rest of the season, much to John's disappointment. The following winter experienced warmer temperatures than normal, so there were no perceptible changes in the glass's structural integrity.

But in 2006, the crack increased in length; in 2007 and 2008, it slowly widened. Finally, during the winter of 2010, the soil above the frost line was much colder than average.

John felt as though he could almost burst the bottle, wax and blood stopper be damned. The winter passed into spring, and he thought he would have to wait through another bitter cycle.

But then, as the spring temperature shot up unexpectedly in May, he heard a dull cracking sound all around him. In a burst of willpower, John exploded out of the glass, causing a soil bubble to erupt above him.

He was free and had regained his physical form, but the air temperature was much too warm for it to be the evening hours. There was little doubt that daylight was shining brightly above him. If he shot out from the ground now, he would burst into orange flame and burn to a cinder; that would be an ironic twist. Death would be overcome with laughter from the sheer joy of it.

So he lay still and waited, although he could barely contain his enthusiasm. It was a pleasure in itself to feel and smell the soil that surrounded him so completely, like a cool blanket. He slowly reached out horizontally, carefully stretching and flexing muscles that had not been tested since the 19th century.

He was so close to the surface now that he could hear children's voices, but they were such a jumble of babbling phrases, requests, and name calling all at once that he couldn't pick up what was actually being spoken. Then he heard the sound of a shrill whistle, and all was silence for several seconds. Finally, a man cleared his throat and spoke up.

'All right, Westchester Putnam Cub Scout Pack 119, quiet down, please. I'd like to introduce you to Mr. Joseph Caputo, our National Park Service Guide for the rest of the day. He is going to fill us in about all of the back and forth fighting that took place here on the second day of the battle, and then we are going to hike to Little Round Top.

After a quick lunch, we will learn about the 20th Maine's desperate charge down the slope of Little Round Top with their commanding officer, Colonel Joshua Lawrence Chamberlain, and the hand to hand fighting that followed.

Remember, when you're done with lunch, I want all of you to look around and police the area so that we follow the scout motto of Leave No Trace. Are we all on board with that, scouts?"

A dozen boys' voices rang out almost simultaneously in a sing song reply: "YEESS, Mr. Paine."

John was surprised by the gentleman's informational pep talk to the children. The battle of Gettysburg was being still being discussed, and appeared to be even studied; and who was this Colonel Chamberlain fellow that the park guide was going to talk about? There was an extraordinary world of the future a few scant feet above him waiting to be explored.

John counted the hours; when the ground became cool and the sounds of voices became that of methodical, chirping crickets, he scooped away the soil with a swimming motion and slowly raised his head to the surface.

He gasped at his first view, a beautiful night sky with bright stars and a shining quarter moon. The sight mesmerized him, and he gazed lovingly at the blue canvas as a soft breeze caressed him with the light smell of grass.

He had no idea how long he lay there taking in his first taste of freedom, but he guessed that the hour was well past midnight. There was not a soul on the battlefield as he rose up from his grave and dusted himself off.

On the ground in front of him was a large shard of the quinine bottle that had been his solitary confinement. He picked it up and rubbed it between his thumb and fore finger, feeling the cool, smooth texture of the glass.

It looked and felt innocent enough, but he wondered how long he would have been able to hold on to his sanity had it not been for the roots that had spread so close to his unearthly prison. He flung the glass against one of the boulders nearby and watched it smash into bits in a dozen directions. How easy that was, now that he was on the OUTSIDE.

But what would this transformation mean to the Vampire Council? Could the destruction of the glass cell be felt by its members now that the Noinjimo had been reversed? Had that ever even HAPPENED before? Were they scrambling to assemble from all parts of the world at this very moment to take up the hunt once more and mercilessly track him down?

He shuddered at the thought of being re-captured at their hands and going through the horror of that incarceration a second time. No one deserved that kind of punishment. He would rather face the emptiness of oblivion.

John decided to put all that aside for the moment. He spread his arms and took to the sky, reveling in the sweet spaciousness all around him as the wind whipped through his hair and pushed it back. It was then that he noticed straight beams of light coming from the direction of Gettysburg. Little did he know that fate would have need of his services one last time.

CHAPTER 12

No Time Like The Present

A glossy black Honda Element cruised out of the Gateway Mini Mart convenience store in Gettysburg onto Steinwehr Avenue and the Emmitsburg Road. The driver took a sip from a can of Budweiser and passed it over to his girlfriend in the passenger seat, who accepted it gratefully with a wink.

"Dawn, I have to say, I had a nice time at your Reliance Mine Saloon tonight. It was great to finally meet and hang out with all of your friends. They're very nice, and the place actually has the feel of being in a tunnel. I really got a kick out of the miner's tools they had around the place."

"Thanks; they liked you, too. I have to admit, you made a good first impression."

"Well, I WAS on my best behavior, and it always helps when I nurse my beers instead of chugging them. It really keeps my head clear."

The woman sighed. "Yes, I have to admit that's a big help, especially in your case. By the way, there's a book signing at the saloon next Saturday night. We should go. Now that the meet and greet with my friends is over and done with, why don't we....BILL, LOOK OUT!"

The car swerved sharply over the double line, off the road onto the grass shoulder, then screeched to a sudden stop just before the post and rail fencing. The shaken couple sprang from the car and ran back to a young man standing alone in the middle of the road with a stupefied expression on his face.

"God damn it! You looked like a baby deer caught in the high beams. What the hell is the matter? You act like you've never seen a car before."

The young man stared at them silently for a moment, and then stammered out a reply. "I...I'm...sorry. I was confused as you...got closer. I really couldn't tell how fast you were coming at me with those lights shining in my eyes."

The young man stared at the car in disbelief, as though he could not comprehend what had just happened. "They were small when I noticed them at first, but then they got bigger and brighter real quick until I couldn't see any more and the next thing I knew you almost...hit me."

"Shit...another foot or less and you would have been splattered around worse than some of those Rebels out here during Pickets Charge."

The man gave a quizzical look while eyeing his near road kill up and down. "Say, that's some outfit you've got on; must have taken you quite some time to find clothes like that. You're a re-enactor, aren't you?

"A re-enactor? Yeees, something like that."

"From the looks of it, you're the spitting image of a bona fide Civil War era sutler. Not many people take an interest in that kind of character. I've got to tip my hat to you on your attention to detail. You've certainly done your research. Are you here for the festivities this weekend?"

"Festivities? Wouldn't miss them for the world."

"Great, well, maybe I'll run into you again. Ah, sorry, poor choice of words. Hope to see you again soon in the daylight mister..."

"Larson...John Larson."

"Larson. OK. My name's Bill Flemming, and this is my fiance Dawn."

The woman smiled weakly and joined in. "It's very nice to meet you, John, I mean, under the circumstances and all. Are you sure you're all right?"

"Fit as a fiddle. Sorry to bother you both. Well, I've got to get going. I want to see what's happening in the town."

She perked up. "Can we give you a lift? It's the least we can do, isn't it, Bill?"

"Sure is; want to hop in and hitch a ride? I promise we won't charge you."

"No...thank you. I prefer to walk, if it's all right with you."

"Suit yourself, but make sure you walk in the grass off the road. You might not be so lucky a second time." The couple walked back into their car and sped off into the night.

John stood and watched them as their red tail lights grew dim and disappeared around a bend in the road. "Son of a bitch," John muttered. He had a lot of catching up to do. That wagon didn't have a single horse pulling it. It was a startling wakeup call for him, no ifs, ands, or buts.

This new time appeared to have the potential to be nearly as dangerous as the one he left behind during the war. The Vampire Council and the Dhampir seem to have been replaced by swift, strange technology that could cause him some major problems if he did not remain on guard at all times.

He followed Bill's advice and walked on the grass shoulder off the side of the road. More cars would pass as he carefully made his way into the outskirts of town. John kept a watchful eye on them all.

These colored boxes seemed to come in many shapes and sizes, but all possessed the deadly significance of speed without the benefit of any horses pulling them. John could only guess that some kind of hidden steam engine propelled them forward.

Businesses lined Steinwehr Avenue as he walked slowly into Gettysburg. At first glance, the town appeared to have prospered while he was imprisoned. The first shop of prominence that drew his attention was a building that looked somewhat like a private home.

It was called The Battle Theatre and General Picket's Buffet, and had four white columns in front, reminiscent of the main house at Etenal Babako, with an American flag hanging proudly from an angled flagpole attached to the second floor facade. But this flag had 50 stars nestled within its waving blue canton. Were there really that many states in the Union now, and where did they all come from?

John had no intention of going inside to sneak a peek, so he assumed that it was a place where one could have a meal and then watch a play about famous battles of the past. He could not understand how the two went together, but by his estimate, he was somewhere in the neighborhood of a century and a half behind the times. Perhaps there were no more wars, and people looked upon the famous ones from antiquity as curiosities.

The next eye catching shop for him was, oddly enough, called KFC. It was a red, one story building with white, horizontal stripes running across it. John thought it unusual that an inn would have initials instead of a name, but stranger still was a larger than life portrait of what looked like a smiling, Southern plantation owner plastered over the front doors. He had bushy white eyebrows, dark glasses, with a smart looking white moustache and goatee.

Entire generations of families were sitting behind glass windows, from grandma and grandpa down to parents and their children, feverishly ripping apart pieces of fried chicken with their bare hands in what looked very much like a piranha feeding frenzy. John almost wished he had a hankering for regular food as stuffed patrons waddled out in a satisfied daze to their conveyances.

He reasoned that Southern food received so enthusiastically in a staunch, anti-slavery town the like of Gettysburg was definitely a sure sign of regional reconciliation. What other logical explanation could there be?

John passed a number of other establishments on both sides of the avenue until he came to the corner of Steinwehr and South Washington Street. There nestled in a triangle shaped area was a one floor, red roofed building with rows of windows all the way around. Affixed to the sloped roof was large white lettering that spelled out the name Tommy's Pizza.

He didn't have the slightest idea what the word pizza meant. He had never even seen or heard the word before now, so his curiosity got the better of him and he wanted to step inside, if he could think of a way. That problem was taken care of immediately.

A small child sitting at one of the tables noticed John's odd dress and waved at him to come in. Hoping that would be an acceptable invitation, John took a chance and opened the door, stepping inside without incident. He waved a thank you back to the child and flashed him a smile.

It turned out that this was yet another eating place, but the smells were unfamiliar to him, and the temperature was surprisingly cold. An aproned cook in the kitchen was removing a round disk from the oven consisting of what looked like slop with a long handled, wooden paddle.

ESCAPE FROM DEVIL'S DEN

"One pepperoni with sausage and peppers" he announced proudly. He put it in a white box and handed it to a waiting customer, who in turn gave him some money while appearing to accept the disgusting creation that was reminiscent of a dog's breakfast with great anticipation.

As the box was being swiftly whisked out the door, a bored, pimple faced lad about 16 years old turned to John from behind the counter and asked blandly "What can I get for you?" He never did get the chance to answer the question. A booming voice from behind John answered for him.

"I'll have two slices with the works and a large Dr. Pepper; my old friend here will have a coffee." John recognized the voice and sighed. It was someone he hadn't heard from for quite some time, not that he was upset.

The boy looked at John and asked "How would you like that coffee?" Once again, the voice piped in.

"He likes his coffee like he likes his women...hot... light...and sweeeet."

The boy gave them both an odd look but proceeded to fill the order as requested. John refused to turn around, but was only postponing the inevitable. The food and drinks were placed on a tray, and the figure stepped forward to pay and take it all away. "This way" he said as they moved to the front of the restaurant and sat in a booth facing each other.

"Well, John; I see that you're none the worse for wear. You don't look a day over 150. How do you do it...moisturizer...gym membership...liposuction?"

John tilted his head to one side like an inquisitive puppy trying to understand a command from its master. "Death, I don't have the slightest idea what you just asked me, but perhaps I'm better off. Gettysburg seems to be your favorite haunt."

"And YOU, John Larson, are my favorite subject. Of course, there IS a cemetery just across the street. You just didn't notice. Anyway, I must admit that you have earned my utmost admiration. No one has ever escaped from the Noinjimo, until now, that is."

Death picked up a slice of gooey, droopy pizza with both hands and began taking huge bites with obvious gusto. "You really should try this. You don't know what you're missing. I call it the garbage slice; it's got something like 10 different toppings, and they're all fresh ingredients."

John looked on impassively. "No, thank you. I'll stick with the coffee. You seem to have adapted effortlessly with the times. What is it you want, besides taunting me incessantly?"

Death brought a hand to his chest and feigned a look of pain. "Why, just to welcome you back and let you know that you're not alone in what is now a unique community. Granted, the place is pockmarked with old buildings, like the counter kid's face over there, but you're in for a quite a shock, just the same."

"Why couldn't I sense that you were behind me just then? I've never had a problem like that before."

"Very simple; Tommy's got the a.c. cranked up tonight."

"And what does a.c. mean? Why are things abbreviated around here now?"

"Air conditioning; greatest invention since the wheel. You're gonna love it, believe me. You'll be impressed with electricity too; that's what's lighting up all these shops and street lamps, in case you were interested."

John got up from the booth, took one long swig of the coffee, and headed for the door without looking back. "Thanks for the warm welcome and pertinent information. It's comforting to know that I have a guardian angel looking out for me. I'm sure we'll bump into each other again...and again...and again. You just can't help yourself."

Death expression turned solemn as he watched John leave the store and walk out onto the busy street. 'No," he whispered, "just... again."

The crowds milling about on Steinwehr Avenue were indeed a Shakespearean witch's brew of players. Anxious parents' herded hyper youngsters scarfing ice cream in front of them like wayward sheep, scruffy teen agers banded together to form obnoxious, moving pockets of babbling noise, and overwhelmed old timers with blank expressions on their faces vainly tried their best to keep up with it all, but only succeeded in clogging up the already crawling, bloated sidewalks.

Occasionally, John noticed that men and young boys in Union and Confederate uniforms would pass amongst the crowd, yet no one would pay them any mind. Women also took part in this charade; several waltzed along in elegant Victorian dresses and hoop skirts topped with delicate white shawls or snoods.

He wondered what would make them dress that way, especially if people barely noticed. Death was right, as usual. This wasn't going to be an easy transformation for him. It was almost like he had awakened in a foreign country.

His first order of business was to find a way to blend in; that meant obtaining new clothes. How he was to do that without acceptable currency was a problem. Theft was an option, even robbery for that matter, but there were no guarantees he wouldn't get caught in the act, and that would shine a spotlight on him and force him to make use of his powers.

John continued walking along busy Steinwehr until he stopped at what looked like a two story house with an attached storefront. A striking blue and white sign off to the side announced that it was The Great T Shirt Company. Curious

onlookers buzzed about the place like flies checking out clothing, souvenirs, and assorted trinkets.

He stood at the picture window and looked inside. There
were racks of brightly colored garments lining the downstairs
room. This was exactly the kind of place he needed to catapult
himself into the present.

But there was an ancient problem; no night creature could
enter a structure without permission. That rule had not
changed since his absence, and there was no child waving him
in this time.

That sticky situation was eliminated with a single, serendipitous glance. Behind the counter in the store an old man sat
bugged eyed while staring up and down at John, then mouthed
frantically for him to come inside. His clothes had done the
trick; lightening had struck twice. John accepted the invitation
and walked through the front door. The introduction, however,
was a bit out of the ordinary.

"Well I'll be dipped in shit if that's not one great outfit,
young man. How long have you been showing that off? It
looks like real homespun."

"Longer than you could imagine."

"My name's Jim Eastwood. I own this place. I couldn't
help but notice that you were looking over at the racks."

"Yes I was; I could do with some new clothes, but I'm a bit
low on funds right now."

The old man smiled broadly. "That might not be as insur-
mountable a problem as you might think. You see my son deals
in vintage Civil War era apparel. I'm sure he'd love to buy what
you're wearing, but unfortunately, he's not here at the
moment."

He stepped out from around the counter and got closer to
John, speaking almost in a whisper. "A lot of the costumes you

see on people walking around outside are decent enough for the everyday re-enactor, but your outfit looks perfect in every detail. Those even look like hand sewn button holes. Would you be interested in selling yours?"

John could have been bowled over with a feather. "You mean...sell you the clothes off my back...right here?"

"RIGHT HERE ANDD RIGHT NOW! Tell you what I'll do. You let me have it all— the shirt, vest, pants, and belt, and I'll give you $250.00. Damn...I didn't notice your boots, boy, and they look in decent shape, too. Throw those in and I'll give you an even $300.00. Whatcha say?"

John was still in a state of shock. "I really don't know WHAT to think, to be perfectly honest with you. You're saying you want all of these clothes for $300?"

"ALL RIGHT! ALL RIGHT! I can see that you're up to snuff about prices on vintage items like these. You can't blame me for trying. Here's the honest poop...I'll give you $300.00, AND you can take any 2 pairs of pants and shirts you want, PLUS a belt and pair of shoes...but ONLY from the sale racks...and NO embroidery. Now THAT'S a good deal, my friend. What do you say to that?"

John raised his eyebrows as his mouth curled into a wide grin. "I'd say...YES!"

CHAPTER 13

Trouble Brewing

"Good evening Companions of Gettysburg; may I have your attention. We are about to re-open the Visitor's Center. Please have your tickets ready so that we can all get safely inside in a timely fashion, then everyone may proceed to the theater for the exclusive showing of the movie."

A buzz went down up and down the line as people simultaneously motioned to their wallets, purses and shirt pockets looking for their entrance passes. One by one, they walked through the glass double doors and dutifully handed their tickets to a waiting receptionist.

The hallway was large and expansive, but the patrons clustered together in anxious anticipation. When the last person was inside, the receptionist waved a fistful of tickets in the air, signaling to the guide that all was in readiness.

"All right everyone; let me first introduce myself. My name is Barbara Babcock and I'd like to thank you on behalf of the Companions of Gettysburg for purchasing these special tickets to the showing of A New Birth of Freedom.

For those of you who are in the building for the first time, this new Visitors Center was opened in April of 2008 as part of a historic and exciting public/private partnership with the

Tinslaye Group and the National Park Service to replace the antiquated, 87 year old Visitors Center that stood on Ziegler's Grove along the Taneytown Road."

The speaker took a breath and glanced around to see that she had everyone's attention. "Construction on the project began in 2005, and the final cost was over 100 million dollars. We feel that this type of relationship is the wave of the future for our national parks. The new Visitors Center is a state of the art facility that all Companions members can be proud of.

Once you have viewed the exquisite 22 minute film, please feel free to browse around at your leisure and take in all of the wonderful new exhibits. There are close to a dozen distinct areas to the museum proper, and I hope that you will take the time to pause and reflect in each and every one of them."

She began to step backward. "Let us now move into the theater to view the film, and then I will be happy to answer any questions that you might have afterwards. Just one more thing; if you listen closely, you will recognize the narrator's voice as belonging to the distinguished actor, Mr. Morgan Freeman. Also during the film you will hear Sam Waterston and Marcia Gay Harden."

An old man in the crowd became confused and turned to his wife. "Marsha, I never heard of Marcia Gay Harden. Who the hell is she? And is Waterston that CSI guy?"

His beet red spouse pulled him along by the arm with the moving crowd into the theater. "That's enough, Fred; this way." The doors slowly closed behind the group, enveloping all but one member. He stayed in the lobby, his eyes riveted on a small collection of rifles inside a glass display case.

A smiling volunteer came up behind him. "Sir, don't you want to see the movie?"

"I've already seen that piece of propaganda bullshit," he said with pent up venom. "In the end, they make it seem to be ALL about slavery."

The smile left the startled young girl's face as she made a fast getaway from the stranger, who continued on alone through the various exhibit areas of the museum. About a half hour later, the group emerged from the theater just as he returned to the lobby. The beaming speaker raised her hands to quiet the murmuring crowd.

"I'm sure that you were all as taken with the film as I was the first time I saw it. Wasn't it absolutely WONDERFUL?" Everyone in the group moved their heads up and down like so many bobble head dolls lined up in the back window of an old Oldsmobile.

"Now, if there are any questions you may have about the new Visitors Center, I will be more than happy to answer them for you." The loner quickly raised his hand.

"Yes, sir, you in the back; what is your question?"

"I have several, actually. My name is Luther Stokes, and I'm from Meadville, Pennsylvania. What I'd like to know is where the hell are the artifacts?"

Babcock shot him a look of disdain and answered icily with her own question. "I don't know what you mean, sir. Will you please be more specific?"

"I sure as hell think you do, lady. I was lucky enough to walk through the old Visitors Center for a number of years, and there were tons of rifles, pistols, and such for everyone to see. Now there's hardly anything here at this new place."

"You don't know what you're talking about."

"No I don't? When the Companions were pushing hot and heavy for this new building with that guy from Tinslaye, all we heard about was how the Park Service had over 35,000 battlefield artifacts rotting away, and what a shame it was that the public wouldn't get to see them before they all fell apart."

"Sir, I don't..."

"Wasn't that why this new place got built? Wasn't that the selling point that all you big shots used in tearing down the other beautiful old Visitors Center? And what do we have now? Dumbed down story presentations with canned speeches, mannequins and stuffed horses." Some in the crowd became angry, but others listened to the man with rapt attention.

Babcock replied with an imperious tone. "Sir, this facility was conceived by some of the foremost minds in the museum community today. I hardly think that your skewed, slanted views have any credible merit whatsoever."

She turned away from him in a huff and addressed the crowd. "Ladies and gentlemen, I am sorry for this uncomfortable episode. Fortunately, we are running out of time. May I have one more question?" A serviceman dressed in an army uniform raised his hand.

"Yes, Ma'am; I have a question. When I was here a few years back, the old Visitors Center had a great electric map that showed how the two armies fought it out over those three days here at Gettysburg. It was a very simple set up by today's standards, but very popular, and I was wondering that since there's so much room here in this new building, is there a possibility that it will be brought back into service any time soon?"

Babcock tried to hide a look of annoyance. "There are no plans at this time to reprise the antiquated electric map. It is currently boxed up in sections and safely stored away."

Stokes ambled over to the soldier and whispered in his ear. "They're afraid they'll have to show it for free; that will cut into the profits on the film. You won't see that map again anytime soon, my friend. The big shots behind the scenes don't like it anymore, and the more people ask about it, the more tone deaf they get."

The speaker gave one last pitch before blending into the crowd. "Feel free to wander around the museum to your hearts' content. It is open exclusively to you First Tier Companions for the rest of the evening." She suddenly remembered something.

"And just a reminder…tomorrow night, there will be a special Cyclorama painting presentation and discussion of celebrated artist Paul Philippoteaux's depiction of Picket's Charge. Believe me, this is an event that you won't want to miss. Tickets are still available for purchase at the Companions main office in the Strepp House on Baltimore Street.

And for goodness sake, please don't forget to complete this evening with a visit to our Refreshment Saloon. A late snack may include tastes of the period food like cornbread, beef stew and chicken pot pie. The Gift Shop will also be open. There you can purchase jewelry, T shirts, drinking mugs, stuffed animals, plus toys and games. The…"

"Excuse me, Ms. Babcock," a shy teenager next to her asked quietly. "But what does all that stuff have to do with the battle of Gettysburg?"

She went on without a hitch. "The book store section is also a must see for your continued Civil War education. If you present your Companions membership card, you will receive a 10% discount on all items purchased. Thank you for your patience and kind attention, and be sure to tell your friends about the benefits of membership in the Companions of Gettysburg."

Polite applause followed, and then people broke up in pairs and small groups to go through the rest of the building. The serviceman shook his head and headed for the door, followed closely by his wife and young daughter. The woman looked concerned. "What's wrong, honey? You look sad."

"I am. When I joined the Companions in the mid 90's, they were in the midst of some great work. Through their efforts, power lines along the Emmitsburg Road were put underground, cannon carriages were re-built, monuments were restored, land was purchased and given to the Park Service, the damned National Tower was finally torn down, and other good things.

But people began to get turned off. It all started with the push for the new Visitor's Center and has gone downhill since. Now the main thrust seems to be public relations, sales, and fund raising. Things went on behind the scenes with this new building that people will never know about, Karen. People can go down a wrong path, and so can organizations.

Well…that's that. Let's head on down to Baltimore Street. We can get tickets for a ghost walk. I promised Lindsay we'd check one out, didn't I Lin?"

"You sure did, Daddy. I thought you'd forgotten. Can I walk between you and mommy on the tour?"

"Absolutely; and after that we can get something cold at the Sunset Ice Cream Parlor."

The happy family walked to the parking lot as their voices faded slowly into the night. They were overheard and watched closely by Luther Stokes, who stood by the side of the entrance. He made a call on his cell phone and waited patiently for the response that came shortly.

"Hello, August? It's me, Luther. Yeah, I'm here in Gettysburg, right at the Visitors Center. I've walked through the building as thoroughly as I could without arousing any suspicion. This fucking place has too many cameras and people moving around. There's no possible way that I could leave something without it being noticed in a few minutes." There was a short pause as Luther waited to hear words of wisdom from his mentor.

"Don't worry about that now, Luther. I just received a juicy piece of information that will make your mouth water. It seems that the descendants of the USCT 29th Infantry Regiment of the Army of the Potomac will be having a reunion and moonlight ceremony at the new Lincoln statue outside the Visitors Center the day after tomorrow. What do you think of that, my friend?"

"That means a lot of niggers in one place at one time. The good Lord is on our side."

"Amen to that Luther; but it also changes the purpose of your mission…to a degree. Rather than destroy the Visitors' Center by itself, do you think you could come up with a plan to damage the building while blowing up those black bastards at the same time?"

"That would be sooo sweeet, August!"

"Indeed it would; and I know that if there's anyone with the ability to do this, it's you. God has placed you there for a reason. Now, what do you think you'll need to make this happen on schedule in two days?"

"The IED's I've got with me are set up special for indoors. They won't do the trick. Now that we're moving the operation to the outside, I'll need to come up with something more combustible and more far reaching. That will be the only way to hit both targets simultaneously with maximum effect."

"Well, you already know when and where they're going to be. That's a big advantage for us."

"Absolutely; all that leaves for me to do is to locate the right spot for placement, and come up with the proper materials. Whatever I use, I should still be able to detonate them via cell phone. In that way, I can be sure of the right moment."

"It sounds like you've already got a handle on things, Luther. I knew that I could count on you. An event like this would be a big morale boost for our brethren all over the United States. Do you need any help?"

"No; the fewest number of people working on this project the better. It will draw less attention. Besides, Jasper's picking up a few things and then hanging back in the room to look after the IED's. The two of us should be able to handle it no problem. I've got to go now; there's more people leaving the Visitor's Center."

"All right, Luther; stay in touch, my man. The Phineas Priesthood is counting on you."

"You got it. I'll call you when I've got everything in place."

Companions Members began to dribble out of the Visitor's Center and down the illuminated flagstone walkway to their cars in the adjacent lots. No one bothered to notice Luther Stokes standing beside a life size bronze statue of a thoughtful looking Lincoln sitting on a stone bench with his famous top hat beside him. But Stokes was not admiring the president; something much more important had caught his eye.

Along the far side of the building, tall, lush rows of emerald green arborvitae stood like silent sentinels. They were an aesthetic screen to hide the cement block portion of the Visitors' Center, but they were also no more than 100 feet from the statue.

For Stokes, it was a dream come true. That particular portion of the building by the shrubs was devoid of any windows. That meant he could go about the business of death and destruction with near invisibility.

There was not enough vertical vegetation around the statue where the reunion would take place, but this location was absolutely perfect. It was situated so that he could target the Visitors' Center AND the ceremony's participants.

What he needed now were the proper materials to accomplish his mission. If all went according to plan, flesh and blood of the people Lincoln freed nearly 150 years ago would be splattered all over his statue.

Luther couldn't help but grin broadly at the supreme irony of the impending situation as he walked briskly to his beat up, faded, red Ford van in the parking lot. The back bumper sported two bumper stickers.

The first was a large Stars and Bars Confederate battle flag, while directly beside it was a rectangular sticker that read:

KEEP HONKING: I'M RELOADING

Stokes knew exactly where he was headed. The van started up with a puff of blue smoke from the tail pipe, pulled out of the lot onto the Baltimore Pike back into Gettysburg, then right onto York Street/Route 30, and straight ahead until he reached his destination, the local Wal-Mart just off of Sixth Street, near the Hampton Inn.

He steered into the lot and turned the engine off, but it continued to chug and convulse several times like a chain smoker in a morning hacking fit before mercifully shutting itself down with a final, choking wheeze.

He got out of the van and stared serenely at the Wal-Mart store in front of him, then mumbled sarcastically to no one in particular; "Ah, the place that has everything…and more!" Stokes picked out a shopping cart that had been left in one of the spaces and made his way inside, steering directly to the Outdoor Living section. He certainly knew his Wal-Marts.

There he picked up four full propane tanks before angling over to the Hardware Section, where he decided on 16 boxes of flat head #8 deck screws. The third aisle was Home Improvement and two cans of green spray paint, plus a roll of duct tape. The final purchase was in Home Electronics for two cell phones.

That would do the trick nicely, he thought proudly. He pulled the cart up to one of the check-out counters and began loading the contents onto the conveyer belt. A senior citizen cashier with a bright yellow "Hello I'm Herb" name tag glanced over at him with a suspicious look.

"That's a strange mix of items you got there, sonny. Whatcha gonna do with all that?" Stokes answered quickly without breaking a sweat.

"Well, I'm just about ready to finish up my new deck with some friends tomorrow, and I thought I'd break it in right by having a big ol' barbeque for them and their families, kinda like a thank you. Oh, those friggin' cell phones are for my kids. They gotta be able to talk to their friends, ya know what I mean?"

"I sure do," the cashier replied with a smile; "All my grand-kids have them, too...wouldn't leave the house without them...just drives their parents up a wall. It's sure not like the old days, that's for damn sure."

The crisis expertly averted, Stokes strolled out to the van with his shopping cart of death and carefully transferred every-thing to the rear storage compartment. A short drive later, he was at the Gettysburg Super 8 Motel parking lot off the York Road.

A quick spray painting of the propane tanks in the back of the van gave him a cheap high just like in the days of his youth. The new green color would blend quite nicely into the arborvi-tae at the Visitors Center.

It was a particularly productive evening for Luther Stokes, proud Phineas Priest. This was a job well done. It was time to crank up the air conditioner and thumb through the newest issue of Guns & Ammo. Now if Jasper Johns was back with the Colt 45 and pork rinds, they could both crack open a few brews and settle in for a good night's sleep.

CHAPTER 14

Strange Revelations

At 9:45 PM, a brank spanking new, 21st century version of John Larson, night creature, emerged triumphantly from The Great T Shirt Company store onto still busy Steinwehr Avenue. He stood resplendent in a light blue J.C. Crew polo shirt, black Levi jeans, a Carhart anvil belt, and a pair of Dockers cordovan loafers.

A white plastic bag of similar items hung loosely from his right hand as he turned to his left and followed a crowd of young college students wearing alternating gray and white Gettysburg College apparel. The students hurried along, and appeared focused on arriving at a pre-determined destination.

Their path eventually led them to a place called O'Rorkes, a white house with green shutters and a picket fence off to the side. John was sure that this was a tavern of some repute. People were even eating and drinking on the property outside, and appeared to be having a good time of it, too.

It seemed to him that although the town of Gettysburg itself had changed over the years, young men and women had not. He felt that to be a good thing. John thought about venturing into the tavern with them, just to satisfy his curiosity. After all, there was a wad of bills totaling $300.00 in his front left pocket, courtesy of the recent clothing swap at The Great T Shirt Company.

Yes, he now had currency AND he blended in with the locals. This was a great start to his new life, but then he remembered that he was long dead, so perhaps a great start to his continued existence would be a more accurate assessment of his situation. He decided not to go into O'Rorkes, and besides, he still needed an invitation.

As he skillfully dodged yapping people who were walking along the sidewalk in both directions at the same time, he strolled nearer to the corner of Steinwehr Avenue and immediately noticed that the old Wagon Hotel had been torn down and replaced with a structure now called The Gateway Mini Mart.

John did not know it, but it was the same store where Bill Flemming and his fiancé Dawn had purchased their Budweisers right before nearly squashing him on the front grill of their Honda.

John thought that although the building looked fairly new, it was no sign of progress by any stretch of his imagination. There was something gaudy and sterile about this building that struck him the wrong way, although people didn't seem to mind as they parked their cars in the lot next to what appeared to be large pumps and then hooked hoses up to them.

He wondered if these new horseless wagons required water to move along; that made sense if his original assessment was correct and they ran on steam.

Much more to his liking was a beautifully kept three story red brick building on the other side the street. It was certainly more in keeping with the true look of 19th century Gettysburg. A large, white oval sign faced out onto Steinwehr Avenue with the inscription: The American History Store etched on it.

On the front door was a notice to all passersby that a number of book signings would take place inside over the course of several days. The next one, scheduled for tomorrow night, was called "The Gettysburg Bicentennial Album," by William Frassanito.

John was fairly certain that not only could he could gain valuable information about the course of the war at this establishment, but quite possibly about subsequent conflicts from around the world as well.

He peeked into the store window to whet his curiosity, and decided that this was definitely a place that he needed to visit in the near future. It maintained an aura of dignity that many of the other businesses sorely lacked.

But it was a house directly across on Baltimore Street that abruptly broke John's train of thought. It was a place that he had long forgotten, but there was someone standing in front of it like a ghost out of the past, his past.

He walked slowly forward until he was standing at the house formerly lived in by Georgia McClellan, a woman he knew well. She was the sister of Jennie Wade, the girl with whom he was smitten so long ago.

In his former life, John had tried to elicit Georgia's help in getting into Jenny's good graces whenever she came into Fahnestocks to do her shopping. The red brick house was not that much different in appearance than he remembered from back in 1863, but there were two glaring changes. The first was a wood routed sign that hung from a gallows-like base; it read:

JENNIE WADE HOUSE MUSEUM

What could that possibly mean? Jennie had lived in a rented house on Baltimore Street; everybody knew that. How could such a mistake have managed to remain undetected over all these years?

The second change was a life sized bronze statue of Jennie herself standing on a granite pedestal. The likeness was unmistakable, even in the half light of the electric torches that Death had spoken of, and John stood in front of it slack jawed and bewildered.

She was staring off into the horizon with a hint of a smile, a loaf of bread in one hand and a pitcher in the other. He did not understand the symbolism of it all until he stepped closer to read the plaque affixed to the pedestal. The inscription read:

Jennie Wade—Age 20 Years Two Months

Killed Here July 3rd 1963

While Making Bread For The Union Soldiers

A further inspection of the house showed that it still bore numerous shell and bullet holes, courtesy of the Rebels within the town. During the battle, John recalled that the McClellan house was actually on the outskirts of Gettysburg, and was close enough to Union soldiers within their defensive line that it would make a tempting target for enemy sharpshooters.

He moved to the side of the house and noticed a small white sign. It contained a child-like drawing of a sheeted ghost, accompanied by the words: Follow The Spirit Into A Haunted House With Ghostly Images. Tour Tickets Sold Here Or Call 965 1245.

He had no idea what to make of that. But as John moved further around the house, he came to a parking lot and another entrance; above it in large white letters was another sign that stated:

JENNIE WADE GIFT SHOP

People were exiting the store with all manner of trinkets and miscellaneous items that John did not recognize. Perhaps it was better that he did not. But then it struck him; his Jennie's death was being used as a way for people to make money. He had been imprisoned for many years, so his Victorian era mindset could not comprehend how someone could do such a thing.

Two things were now certain to him; he existed in a graceless age, and the employees of this establishment were very fortunate that he had lost major portions of his human emotions.

John was contemplating his next move when a small gathering of about 10 people emerged from the back of the house following what appeared to be the group's leader. They stopped by the gift shop entrance and waited patiently as he summed up.

"So there you have it, ladies and gentlemen. On the morning of the third day of the battle, as 20 year old Jennie was selflessly kneading bread in the kitchen of her sister's home for hungry Union soldiers, a Rebel mini ball pierced through the wood of two doors and struck her in the back. The fatal bullet passed through her heart, and she was killed instantly. Union soldiers wrapped her in a blanket, and she was placed temporarily in the basement of the house, accompanied by her family.

By the way, the kitchen is very much the same as it was when Jennie made use of it in 1863, and the bullet holes in the doors speak for the stark finality and indifference of war. Can you imagine sitting there in that dark basement listening to the sounds of battle above you, right next to the dead body of your daughter?

That's exactly what Jennie's mother Mary had to endure on July 3rd. And yet, this extraordinary woman continued to make bread for the soldiers despite her grievous personal loss."

The guide raised his hands in what was to be a final appeal. "Now don't forget; for those not of the faint of heart, please return tonight at 11PM so that we can we explore the Jennie Wade House, and be inside at the stroke of midnight in search of her restless spirit, which is said to remain here.

Many people have experienced uncomfortable sensations while touring the house, and cameras have picked up a number of anomalies such as floating orbs and strange streaks in their photos."

He looked around slowly with an expression of both surprise and fear. "Could it be Jennie attempting to reach out to us? Perhaps the suddenness of her death was so swift and traumatic that her spirit cannot come to grips with her own death. But I will ask the question that you are all thinking about, but will not speak of it. DARE we go into the BASEMENT later tonight?"

The man exhaled. "Thank you again, ladies and gentlemen. Tickets for tonight's midnight tour, which runs for about 90 minutes, can be purchased at Ghostly Images of Gettysburg at 777 Baltimore Street. Ticket prices for the tour are $10.00 for adults and $5.00 for children under 12 years of age.

That concludes this tour. Remember, the gift shop is still open for some last minute souvenirs and collectibles for your entire family. I hope to see you back here later tonight, and enjoy the rest of your stay here in Gettysburg and Adams County."

Obligatory clapping was heard from the group before it began to disperse in all directions. An older woman grabbed hold of her husband's arm and walked away with a question of her own. "Wait a minute; Tom, isn't there a special price for senior citizens?"

Her weary spouse answered sarcastically from years of habit. "No, Anne. They really don't want seniors on the trip, dear. It's too scary; they're afraid that some old geezer will get a heart attack and become a permanent fixture on the tour. Besides, you're half asleep already."

"Oh my," the woman replied with indignation. "They should tell people our age about that up front. There are laws in this country protecting senior citizens from business predators.

There was a man on Channel 2 News talking about it the other night."

Yeeess, you're right," the husband exhaled with a tinge of humorous despair. "Say goodnight, Gracie."

John had listened and watched attentively during the entire summation. It was all he needed to know about the fate of the girl he had loved so long ago. But he could feel no real pain; it was more like an annoyance. This was one time that being a night creature turned out to be a good thing.

He entertained the idea of buying a ticket for the midnight tour, but thought the better of it and decided to move on. What if Jennie's spirit WAS still in the house? She would surely single him out, and thus draw attention to him, a mistake of huge proportions. He had to make sure he remained blended into the crowds.

John passed a massive building next door to the house. A large brown and green sign out in front declared it to be:

The 1863 Inn Of Gettysburg

Underneath, a smaller white sign with black lettering strangely announced:

Join Our Loyalty Program & Enjoy Instant Savings

He could not imagine that the United States government was still requiring Loyalty Oaths, AND in a Union state after nearly 150 years, with the war long over, but there it was for everyone to see. There must be a reason for that, and he was determined to find out what it was in the coming days. Were some Southerners still fighting the war in their hearts?

John ventured across the road and walked along Baltimore Street towards the town square until he stopped just short of the corner at South Street. He stared at the red brick house in front of him. It was a place he knew well in his previous life. The

Sweney family owned it and lived there during his time in Gettysburg.

Sweney family owned it and lived there during his time in Gettysburg.

Before the war, John would occasionally drop off sundries from Fahnestocks to Mrs. Sweney, who would reward him with delicious baked goods that never failed to satisfy. She was an outstanding cook, and he looked forward to these excursions with great anticipation. But cake was no longer on the menu for John; that time was gone forever. A tall pole with triangular sign and a small, decorative roof over it proclaimed:

FARNSWORTH HOUSE DINING

Another oval shaped sign hung below it and off to the side read:

VICTORIAN BED & BREAKFAST

The house was fronted by a dry stone wall with decorative railing, and complemented by lush ground ivy. An open brook ran by the side of the house and then disappeared underground, but a curving red brick walkway revealed weathered pergolas and a quiet courtyard with sitting areas decorated with an assortment of garden ornaments.

A further look revealed a red sign attached to the bricks on the side of the house that read:

FARNSWORTH TAVERN

It had an arrow pointing left towards an entrance door. Now THIS was an establishment that tweaked John's curiosity. He decided to make the tavern the place where he would break the ice and begin to mingle in with the natives, so to speak. If there was anywhere that he might find a good place to figure out just what going on in this new world, it would be right there.

But first, he had one more stop to make. He continued down Baltimore Street until he came to the home of his cousins, Henry and Catherine Garlach. It was still standing, with mod-

141

est alterations, but it was definitely their old, red brick house. To the left of the house, close to the alleyway leading to the back-yard, was a metal stand with photographs of several people, along with an inscription.

John recognized the people immediately; they were his cousin, Catherine Garlach, and the cowering general he had nearly killed in a fit of rage. Below that picture was a name; it read: Brig. Gen. Alexander Schimmelfennig, Union 11th Corps. So that was the bastard, John thought to himself. What did this marker mean? He glanced up at the heading and read:

A UNION GENERAL ESCAPES CAPTURE

In 1863, this building to your right was the home of cabinetmaker Henry Garlach and family.

Cut off during the Union retreat to Cemetery Hill, General Alexander Schimmelfennig was able to avoid capture by the Confederates, when he hid here for 3 days in the back-yard, shielded behind a stack of firewood and a hog slop barrel situated along the front of the kitchen woodshed.

General Schimmelfennig was sustained with food and water secretly delivered to him by Mrs. Catherine Garlach, when she went to feed the family hogs.

So dear sweet Catherine had been singled out for her bravery and compassion after all. John was satisfied that she had been given her due; supremely happy was no longer in his vocabulary or his emotions. He also hoped that General Schimmelfennig was stripped of his rank after the truth about his choice of hiding places was made known.

How strange was it that two of the most unlikely people would be joined at the hip of history? No matter now; it was time to head on back to the Farnsworth Tavern to discover what people of this century were REALLY like.

CHAPTER 15

Belly On Up To The Bar

J ohn actually began to feel a tiny spark of excitement as he made an about face on Baltimore Street and worked his way back to the Farnsworth House Tavern. It was the best that he could muster. When he reached the corner of South Street, there was a crowd mingling in front of the inn. A free standing, A-frame sign on the sidewalk announced:

FARNSWORTH HOUSE GHOST WALK

He noticed the leader of the crowd was a young man who was wearing clothes that were not unlike the ones he had just traded in at The Great T Shirt Company, only much cleaner. John decided to listen in for a moment. First it was the Jennie Wade Museum, and now this. Why were people here obsessed with spirits? The gentleman was set to begin, and he wasted no time barking out his spiel.

"All right, ladies and gentlemen, let's get this show on the road, shall we? My name is Bart Linehan, and I'd like to thank you on behalf of the Farnsworth House for purchasing tickets for this ghost walk. As I move amongst you, please have your tickets ready so that we can begin our walk this evening. Tonight's topic will be Confederate Hospitals in the town."

Linehan snatched tickets left and right as he wriggled his way around the standing figures in the darkness. As he got to John, he noticed that he did not have a ticket and appeared to make a mental note of it.

"This is my fourth year performing these ghost walks, so I have a lot of information to relay to you tonight." He finished his collection and maneuvered back to the front of the group.

"That about does it; thank you for your patience. As I just said, tonight's walk will be about Confederate Hospitals here in Gettysburg. I am sure some of you know that Baltimore Street was flooded with injured soldiers after three days of intense battle. There was hardly a house on the street that did not have red flagging of some sort to indicate that wounded soldiers were being treated inside.

Unfortunately for the Rebels, when Lee retreated back to the safety of Virginia, he was forced by logistical concerns to leave hundreds of incapacitated Southern boys in the hands of the enemy.

But they were not turned aside by the good townspeople of Gettysburg. In truth, many residents put their political and personal sentiments aside and opened their homes and even their hearts to them. It was a magnificent demonstration of compassion, to be sure.

Now if you would all walk this way, I will start by telling you about young Tillie Pierce, a teenage girl who witnessed a great deal of suffering, and then talk about some restless spirits that have remained in their temporary hospitals to this very day.

Please watch your step and mind the cars when we cross. The local college students usually drive in a hurry, and don't like waiting for people in the streets for very long periods of time.

Forewarned is forearmed, I always say, and if you enjoy this tour, we have others that may interest you as well. There is the Cemetery Hill Tour, the Gettysburg College Tour, the Mature

ESCAPE FROM DEVIL'S DEN

Tour for adults only, and the Ghost Hunt, where we supply equipment that is used to gather the sights and sounds of the supernatural."

John watched as the group slowly trekked off, and was about to continue to his destination when he noticed a long line of people waiting patiently by the inn's entrance steps. He sidled up to the front of the line to question the first person.

The middle aged man appeared to be accompanied by his younger wife or girlfriend. She suddenly wrapped her arms around him and gave him a long, passionate kiss on the mouth; at that moment John surmised it could not possibly have been the man's wife.

He had a funny feeling that this was another spook hunt of some sort; he had to ask. "Excuse me, sir; I couldn't help but notice the line of people behind you and I was curious to know if this is some sort of...I don't know how else to say it...a ghost party?"

"Why, in a way, yes it is. This is the Farnsworth House's Mourning Theatre. A storyteller takes us into the darkened basement of the inn and goes through a list of ghost stories that took place here. There were even a couple of Rebel bodies stored down there for a while. We did this last year and had a great time."

His female partner quickly gave him a sharp elbow to the midsection, doubling him over. "What's this WE shit?" she screeched. "This is my first time here with you."

Before the startled man could catch his breath and bluster out a reply, John thought it best to move on to the tavern. He was a bit taken back by her words and actions. At least women in his past life had some measure of decorum, to put it mildly.

As he made his way past the line of waiting people, a bratty young boy of about 10 at the very end looked up at him with an attitude and asked in a smarmy whine: "Hey, aren't you going into the basement with us, mister? Don't you believe in the supernatural...or are you just a chicken?" He put his hands under his armpits and flapped his arms up and down. "Bock, bock, bock!"

John pretended to be shocked. "You mean ghosts... witches... zombies...and werewolves? There's no such thing, you know that, don't you?"

The boy sneered in disgust; "Maybe, but what about vampires? You didn't mention vampires, LOOOOSERR!"

John instantly tired of the little cretin. He glared, looked him squarely in the eyes, and produced a wide, toothy grin with an ominous reply in a near whisper. "Ask me no questions, I'll tell you no lies."

The youngster froze briefly in silent fear with his mouth as wide as a Dunkin Donut. There would be no more wisecracks forthcoming tonight. To his oblivious parents, who were busy chatting up another couple in front of them, the brief conversation with John would wind up working better than their standard Bailey's in the chocolate milk trick.

Finally, John reached the front door to the inn, and then stopped. In his haste to find out about the revelers inside, he had almost forgotten the night creatures' ancient and annoying rule of entry. How was he to get someone to invite him inside?

The problem was solved in a flash. No sooner had he planted himself outside the front door, when it opened, and a very inebriated young man stared at him; their eyes locked.

"Well," the stranger slurred slowly, "make up your mind, chief. Are you goin' inside or not? I don't have all night. You waiting for an invitation?"

John perked up and sensed an opportunity; "Yes; could you supply me with one?"

The man laughed and moved to the side with a bow and a magnificent swooping hand gesture. "Absolutely; go on in, your highness. Your subjects await your presence with bated breath."

It was as simple as that. John shook the man's hand and stepped over the threshold to what appeared to be a cramped alcove with a ramp leading to another door. As he made his way up the ramp he heard the lighthearted buzz of people evidently having a good time.

He opened the door; straight ahead were happy patrons sitting and standing in front of a long bar. John spied an open stool and sat down in his first tavern in many a year.

It actually felt good. He leaned forward and put his elbows over the bar rail. In spite of his long lost desire for food, he still wanted the taste of beer in his mouth, sliding down his throat. The bartender, a barrel chested, jovial looking man with a large black beard, saw John without a drink and made his way towards him. He wore a Boston Red Sox T shirt stretched out over his ample belly.

"Good evening, friend, what can I get for you tonight? You look like a fella who could use a drink."

"Does it show that much?" John asked in a surprised tone. "I'd LOVE a beer."

"We've got em' all; Bud, Beck's, Miller, Sam Adams, Coors, Yuengling, Rolling Rock, Killian's, Blue Moon…"

"I'll try the Blue Moon" John interrupted. He took out two $20.00 bills and put them on the bar, not knowing how much items cost now.

"Coming right up; the name's Paul McGann." He stretched his hand out over the bar. John hesitated for a moment, and then shook it firmly.

"John Larson; pleased to meet you."

"Damn, John, your hand's freezing. You sure you don't want some hot coffee instead?"

John smiled. "No, thank you. The beer will be fine."

"Comin' right up; here's a menu if you're hungry."

John picked up what looked like a long, tan covered pamphlet. The front cover showed two soldiers standing at attention under the words: THE HISTORIC FARNSWORTH HOUSE TAVERN MENU. He opened it and began to read the first page with great interest.

> *Welcome to the historic Farnsworth House Inn. The house is named in honor of Brigadier General Elon Farnsworth, who led an ill-fated charge after the failure of Pickets Charge, claiming the lives of Farnsworth and 65 of his men.*
>
> *The original part of the house was built in 1810, followed by the brick structure in 1833. The house sheltered Confederate sharpshooters during the three day conflict, one of whom it is believed accidentally shot 20 year old Mary Virginia "Jennie" Wade, the only civilian who died during the battle. More than 100 bullet holes pock the walls.*
>
> *Following the battle, the house served as a hospital. The Lincoln procession passed the Farnsworth House on November 19th, 1863, on the way to the National Cemetery, where he delivered the famous Gettysburg Address.*
>
> *The Farnsworth House is in good company. It has the same distinction as the Hotel del Coronado in San Diego, the Queen Mary Hotel in Long Beach, and the Lizzie Borden Bed and Breakfast in Fall River. What's the connection? They are all among the most haunted locations in America.*

John had unintentionally picked up a treasure trove of back history smack in the middle of a public house. So his poor Jennie's fatal bullet came from this very place, most probably the garret, if his sense of topography and geometry was still up to snuff. And Mr. Lincoln had come to give a great speech at some new cemetery set up somewhere on the outskirts of the town. Who would have imagined that the President would come here?

But that preoccupation with ghosts kept popping up everywhere in this town. The residents seemed obsessed with the subject. Fortunately, a scan of the opposite page relayed a different storyline.

Listed under Specialty Drinks and Spirits were: the Louisiana Tiger Fire, the Robert E. Lee Cooler, Old Pete's Punch, Confederate Sharpshooter, the Red Rebel Yell, and a drink named the Scarlett O'Hara, whoever that was.

Perhaps she was a famous prostitute. John could not decide if someone was being sarcastic or just flat out silly. He thumbed through the rest of the menu and saw nothing of informational value until he reached the back page.

Across most of the page was a photo of various articles of military clothing and accoutrements protected behind a glass case, along with an explanation of just what was so important. The caption under the picture stated:

> Our free display of memorabilia from the movie Gettysburg was purchased in 1992 from Turner Network. It represents the largest Gettysburg movie collection to be seen anywhere. The tavern was designated during the filming as the official "officers club". Tom Berenger (Longstreet) and Sam Elliot (Buford) frequented the tavern as well as the entire movie staff. Posters are on display signed by the staff in its entirety.

He turned around in his chair and directly behind him was the very clothing he had just read about. It all looked to be in excellent condition; how that was possible was beyond him, with the war fought so long ago. That word movie was the key. It had to signal some new development that had taken place since his imprisonment.

"Here's your Blue Moon, John; that'll be $3.50." The bartender took one of John's $20.00 bills and rang up the sale, returning the rest.

"Thank you. I'm really going to enjoy this." John put the bottle to his lips and took several gulps, swigging the brew around in his mouth before swallowing it while closing his eyes. "Boy that's good!" He dropped his head back, opened his mouth and let out a long sigh, but his relaxation was short lived.

"God damn but you've got great teeth, dude…especially the incisors. Did you have them all bonded?"

John tensed up and shifted quickly to his right, not knowing what to expect. Sitting next to him was a balding, middle aged man with piercing blue eyes, but his demeanor was anything but confrontational. In fact, the man had every appearance of being serenely drunk.

John relaxed and took a sip of his beer. "Isn't that an odd question to ask a stranger, mister…"

The man chuckled and clapped his hands together. "Canterino, Joe Canterino; yeah, I guess it's strange, but it goes with the territory. I'm a dentist… got a practice over in York. The wife and kids are away visiting relatives in Connecticut so I thought I'd stop by the Tavern for a few. Have you ever been to York?"

"Not for quite some time, I'm afraid," John replied. He looked up and over the dentist's shoulder, and was suddenly hypnotized. In a large rectangular box just below the ceiling was a picture of a man at a podium with American flags behind him on either side. This man was giving a passionate speech and gesticulating with his hands.

Because of the noise in the tavern, John could not hear what was being said, but the picture was definitely moving.

That was it, he thought; today they could somehow make pictures that actually moved! He could not comprehend how that was possible, but seeing was believing. A closer look showed the well-dressed, handsome figure in the picture to be a light skinned black man.

But what was even more astonishing than the moving picture itself was the round insignia attached to the front of the podium. It was the image of an eagle, with an olive branch in one claw and arrows in the other. In its beak it held a white ribbon that read **E Pluribus Unum**, and all the way around the outer portion of the circle were words that read **Seal of the President of the United States**.

John's mouth dropped, once again revealing his gorgeous teeth to the admiring dentist. "I don't believe it! A Negro is President of the United States of America!"

Canterino winced, then cracked a smile. "It does makes people stop and think how far we've come, but be careful there, my friend. The politically correct terminology today is African American. You always have to be on the lookout for the word police these days; they're everywhere, and if you don't use terminology they like, then you're a racist."

"Why isn't anyone here paying any attention to what the President is saying?"

"They don't need to; it's just the same load of horseshit he's been peddling for the last two and a half years since he's been in office: everything is Bush's fault, all Republicans are country club fat cats who hate minorities, and we need to pay more taxes so he can enact more government programs that will accomplish nothing but buy votes for the Democrats and add to the national debt.

God, what a fucking mess, and we've gone something like 12 plus months of 400,000 new people filing for unemployment benefits. The real sad part to all this is that the media continues to make excuses for this phony and give him a free pass.

You heard of John Gotti, the teflon don? Well, say hello to Barack Obama, the teflon President."

Canterino exhaled and dropped his head. "Sorry about spouting like that, but people today are either stupid or blind."

He picked up his glass of Bass Ale and stared at it sadly. "Personally, I think they're just assholes and ideologues...but that's only MY opinion. What do I know anyway? I stick my fingers in peoples' mouths all day. By the way, I didn't get your name."

John's head was spinning. It appeared that taverns were the place to find out what was going on in the country today. He would definitely have to visit another to get more current information.

He got up and slapped the dentist on the back; "John Larson...nice talking to you, doc." He drained the Blue Moon and picked up the rest of his money, leaving a $2.00 tip. As he made his way to the exit, he passed a young man standing at the bar next to a pretty young girl seated beside him.

John could smell the testosterone building in the man's body, so he knew what this fellow was up to. The man reached for something in his back pocket, then put it next to the unsuspecting girl and tapped her gently on the shoulder. She turned around with a hard look of suspicion, and he asked in a quiet, respectful tone "Excuse me miss, but does this bandana smell like chloroform to you?"

The girl blinked, stared for a moment, and then burst into laughter. She snatched the bandana from his hand and gave it a whiff. "No, it doesn't, but that line was so bad that I think you should buy me a beer, don't you?"

The young man smiled, motioned to the bartender for more drinks, and edged closer to her. John could not believe what he had just witnessed. Did women of today actually enjoy introductions of that sort? Adapting to this century was going to require more patience than he thought.

The incident convinced him that it was time to leave, but then it struck him that he had no place of refuge! The Garlach House was no longer safe. He did not know if it was inhabited, and there was way too much foot traffic. The odds that the Gatehouse was still standing after all these years were slim, or were they?

John was up against the clock. It would be daylight in a few hours, and he needed one and possibly two locations that he could rely on for sleep and safety. In his desire to investigate his new surroundings, he had neglected the most basic of needs. Walking was now out of the question. He needed stealth and speed.

He decided to follow his nose. He crossed Baltimore Street and continued on until he reached a semi secluded area with several adjoining buildings. A quick look at the white lettering on one read Eisenhower Elementary School. He walked behind a jut out and took to the sky.

After all those years of being entombed by the Vampire Council, John now relished the simple joy of gliding through the night air. He followed the Baltimore Pike for a short way until he saw his destination in all its glory—the Evergreen Cemetery Gatehouse. Not only was the building still standing, it had been meticulously cared for.

When last John viewed the Gatehouse, all of its windows had been broken, and the surrounding area was pockmarked from the proximity of war. Now, the building and grounds looked as though loving hands had rescued it all from the edge of destruction.

He touched down on the northern section of the Gatehouse roof. The hatch door to the crawlspace was still there, although now it was made of metal, and the roofing material had been had been replaced and re-tarred.

He took hold of the door handle and gave it a slight tug. The hatch continued to open on its own, courtesy of an attached

153

piston rod. John was impressed; he got down on his knees and lowered his head into the attic crawlspace. It was not much different, except that old junk had now been replaced with new junk.

There was still enough room for him to lie down; that was the important thing. Before slipping inside, he walked over to the ledge and looked around. The tent that Elizabeth and her family used as a makeshift shelter was long gone, but he spied something odd nearby. It was a statue.

When he was fairly certain that no one was around, John vaulted over the edge to the ground and approached a bronze figure. It was of Elizabeth Thorne.

She was standing erect with her left hand wiping her brow while holding a shovel with her right arm against her body. But the most telling thing John noticed was that Elizabeth was visibly pregnant. He remembered that she and her parents had many burials to perform, but the delicacy of her condition made her tasks all the more noteworthy, and noble.

Then again, John was not surprised at her being remembered so fondly after all these years. She was that kind of woman, but he wondered about the condition of her unborn child. A circular granite apron acted as the base of the statue, and it was surrounded by a bed of red and white begonias.

One thing was for certain; the Civil War and its participants both civilian and military had not been forgotten, at least in the town of Gettysburg. He wondered if it was that way at all of the other battle sites around the country. No matter; dawn was creeping silently over the landscape. It was time for John to rest before pondering his next move.

CHAPTER 16

Sinister Plans

"I just don't think that's how the few last notes go. I know MY drum beat for the whole song, but if you want to be a real fifer, you'd better get hold of Uncle Joe so he can show you how to finish it up properly."

"What makes YOU so smart all of a sudden? Just stick to your drum sticks, OK? I ought to know my own instrument."

The two young re-enactors sat on the grass and argued back and forth amidst the living history encampment in front of the American Civil War Museum on Baltimore Street. A well-dressed black soldier with sergeants' stripes heard the commotion and walked slowly towards them, assessing the situation.

"Now hold it there a minute, you two. We are out here to show people how Company F of the 29th Infantry Regiment, United Sates Colored Troops conducted themselves during the war. Do we really want them to see the company's fifer and drummer boy arguing about a tune?" The boys lowered their heads in embarrassment.

"Now, I want you both to practice Battle Hymn of the Republic and Yankee Doodle separately...and then together. We want to look smart in front of the Lincoln Statue for the ceremony, don't we?"

"Yes, Uncle Joe, we do; we're sorry, and don't worry, we'll get it all straightened out."

"Good!" Uncle Joe turned and walked back towards his campsite. "I know I can count on you. And by the way, Curtis, Andrew did play the last few notes of Liberty Tree correctly."

Andrew's face turned to sublime victory. "Told you, suckah," he whispered. "Now let's take turns with Battle Hymn. You go first while I chill a bit." He placed his hands behind his head, closed his eyes, and lay flat on the ground waiting to hear the drum beat of his cousin.

But he never heard a sound. After a few moments, he opened his eyes to see a scruffy, bearded, good ol' boy standing over him with a scowl on his face. Before Andrew could sit up, the man made his right hand into the shape of a pistol and pointed it directly at him while he recited one of his favorite movie scenes.

"I know what you're thinking. Did he fire six shots, or only five? Well, to tell the truth, in all this excitement I kind of lost track myself. But being as this is a .44 Magnum, the most powerful handgun in the world, and would blow your head clean off, you've got to ask yourself one question: Do I feel lucky? Well...do ya, PUNK?"

The boys burst out laughing. Curtis chirped in. "Hey, mister, I know where that's from; it's from Dirty Harry. Clint Eastwood said that when he stopped those bad guys from robbing a bank."

"You're right, boys; Mister Dirty Harry Callahan himself. Now there's a fella who knew how to set things right." The man started walking slowly down Baltimore Street.

"You two go on and practice your tunes and have a nice day, hear?" He continued walking past the encampment and stopped in front of KFC, staring inside the store window. Just a few minutes later, another man strode out carrying a bucket of chicken in one hand, and a white plastic bag filled with side orders in the other. He was not happy.

"Let me take a wild guess; you went up to the encampment didn't you? What did I just finish telling you this morning about drawing attention to yourself, Jasper? You don't use your fuckin' head sometimes."

"I was just playin' around with the little Sambos, Luther. Boy, I would have loved to just blow their fuckin' brains out all over the place. Besides, I did some snoopin' around while I was at the encampment and overheard some good shit.

They're still set for their moonlight ceremony two nights from now at the Visitor Center's Lincoln Statue. Everybody's just waitin' on an OK from one of the hot shot speakers from the Department of the Interior to free up his schedule and give a speech; then everything will be all set."

"And we'll be all set to scatter them in every direction you can think of. You can count on it. Let's get back to the room. I want to have lunch, check on the equipment, and make sure to call August with an update."

"He sure likes to know what's goin' on, doesn't he?"

"There's a lot ridin' on this assignment, Jasper. If we can pull this sucker off, it'll be NATIONAL NEWS, my man. Think about it, with just one explosion we can off a bunch of shines, fuck up the Visitor's Center, AND get rid of the new Lincoln Statue, sort of like an icing on the cake."

Jasper's eyes locked on Luther as he rambled on. "A victory like this could be a big draw for the cause; more money comin' in, new members, and rattlin' the cages of some of those ass-holes who keep screamin' "Diversity Diversity" like a bunch of goddamn mynah birds. Yeah, this is big all right, and we're gonna be the ones to do it."

"All right then Luther. Let's get back to the hotel. I'm starved."

The two drove in silence back to the Super 8 Motel. Charlie Daniels' The Devil Went Down To Georgia blared on the radio as they pulled into the parking lot, exited the car with their food stash and made a bee line for their first floor room.

Eating fried chicken while lying propped up on the beds was the first order of the afternoon. Jasper turned on the television and started channel surfing as his partner dove into the bucket like a shark scarfing a harp seal.

"Holy shit, Luther; we're in luck. This is one of my favorite old Star Trek episodes."

"I can't watch that crap; it's too complicated. Why don't you find ESPN? They're gonna have the Brickyard 400 on later this afternoon. We might even get a chance to scope out Danika Patrick."

"Fuck that; here comes the really good part. Listen to this put down, Luther."

"All right Spock, you mutinous, disloyal half-breed, we'll see about you deserting my ship."

"The term half-breed is somewhat applicable, Captain, but computerized is inaccurate. A machine can be computerized, not a man."

"What makes you think you're a man? You're an overgrown jackrabbit; an elf with a hyperactive thyroid."

"Jim, I don't understand..."

"Of course you don't understand. You don't have the brains to understand. All you have is printed circuits."

"Captain, if you will excuse me."

"What else would you expect from a simpering, devil eared freak, whose father was a computer and whose mother was an encyclopedia?"

"My mother was a teacher; my father an ambassador."

"Your father was a computer, like his son...from a planet of traitors. The Vulcan never lived to have an ounce of integrity."

"Jim, please don't..."

"You're a traitor from a race of traitors. Disloyal to the core; rotten like the rest of your sub-human race, and you've got the GALL...to make love to that girl. Does she know what she's getting, Spock; a carcass full of memory banks who should be squatting on a mushroom, instead of passing himself off as a man. You belong in a circus, right next to the dog-faced boy."

Jasper clicked off the television with the remote. "Come on, Luther; admit it...wasn't that SWEEEET? That's exactly how I felt when I was going through the encampment this morning, like I was walking in the middle of a jungle full of animals."

"I hear ya Jasper." Bits of chicken parts flew from his mouth onto the bed spread and floor. "We're gonna take care of that feelin' once and for all, but right now, we need to set up these cell phones."

Luther picked them out of the Wal Mart bag and tossed one to his partner. "The worst part is trying to get the hard plastic wrapping off these mutherfuckers. The propane tanks are ready to go. After we tape one cell phone and the boxes of screws to them in the van, all we gotta do is place them tonight at the Visitor's Center, attach the electrical firing circuits to the base transceiver, and then dial her up whenever we want."

"How close am I gonna be Luther? I sure as hell don't want to be no lateral damage."

"That's collateral damage, asshole. Relax; I'll be in my car in the parking lot. You'll be just on the main pathway leading to the Visitors Center, with a view of both me and the ceremony.

When you hear the speech starting up, they'll start bunchin' up around the statue.

That's when you walk towards me nice an easy like, and when I see you tip your cap, I make the phone call and...BOOM! Let the weepin' n' gnashin' begin...while we drive away as smooooth as silk and watch the first responders race past us on the road."

"Sounds like the real deal, Luther. I'm glad that August hooked me up with you."

"He did that so you can learn how to do things the right way. Now stuff your face while I give him a call, and be sure to keep quiet."

Luther got up off the bed and started towards the bathroom.

"Damn it Luther; you ate the thighs and legs and left me nothin' but the fuckin' wings. That ain't right."

"I'm dialing...I left you all of the mashed potatoes and gravy, didn't I? So shut the fuck up...No! Not you, August. I was just talkin' to Jasper.

We're in pretty good shape down here. We have everything we need, and we'll plant our charges sometime after midnight. It's a pretty good bet that there's no one around the Visitor's Center at that time. If there is, we'll just have to be careful and go to stealth mode."

"Luther, I want you to make sure you keep a close eye on Jasper. He means well, but he's new to the Priesthood. I'm not sure how he'll react under pressure the first time around."

"Don't worry August. I've got everything under control. Have you got any more intel for me?"

"Yes, the ceremony is still slated for 9PM tomorrow evening. The representatives from the Interior Department have confirmed it in interdepartmental e-mails. Some asshole Undersecretary in a blue suit and an American Flag pin on his lapel is set to fly in. I never even heard of him before; must be some jerk weed bean counter stepping out of his cubicle for a breath of fresh air."

"How the hell do you know all this?"

"I'm not at liberty to tell you that, Luther; just make sure everything is set on your end."

"Gotcha; do you want me to get back to you?"

'No...if there's a problem, I'll call you; otherwise, don't contact me again. The fewer cell phone calls with me the better. Who knows what random chatter the Feds pick up with all those goddamn satellites flying around up there? I wouldn't be surprised if they monitor the White House crappers to see who farts the loudest."

"I understand; what about AFTER we blow them up?"

"You just follow the map locations I gave to you before you left; that will put you in enough safe houses until you get back home. Give Jasper his map after the event. He'll have a different route from you."

"Does he know mine?"

"No, I don't trust him enough yet, that's why I kept him in the dark. You're one of my lieutenants; he's a private; get my meaning?"

"I sure do. Hopefully, there'll be no changes and I'll see you in about a week."

"Bless you, Luther; remember...we are here to stamp out the stinking pestilence all around us so white people can take their rightful place once again at the head of our society, steering this country straight."

"When are you gonna contact the media?"

"I'm not going to do anything of the kind. The Priesthood was originally set up for individuals to act on their own accord when and where they saw an opportunity. I'm trying to build up a command structure again so that we can coordinate our efforts and do more damage.

No need for publicity, and the scrutiny that goes along with it. I want to fly under the radar for the time being. It'll get out there quick enough on its own to the people we want to recruit."

"Maybe the media will think it's those Iranian camel jockeys again."

"Not a chance; even if the Feds thought it were true, they'd make up some excuses and then hush it up. Mr. Barack Hussein Obama doesn't want his brothers smeared in any way, just like they're pussyfooting around with that Fort Hood guy.

They're not even saying that the incident is a goddamn terrorist attack! They're claiming that it's nothing but workplace violence, can you believe it? The son of a bitch is guilty as sin, but all you see on the nightly news is that this is an isolated incident that has nothing to do with radical Islam.

What a total load of shit. Obama's got to keep that Muslim outreach going no matter how many Americans it kills."

A quick exhale followed and he began to contain his composure. "Anyway, I've got to go. You're doing the Lord's work, Luther; keep that in mind at all times."

"Amen, Brother."

CHAPTER 17

Cyclorama Drama

J ohn opened his eyes and took a deep breath. Although the items stored within the attic crawlspace of the north Gatehouse had long since changed, the actual smell of the building itself seemed to remain the same after so many years. It must have been the bricks and wood effortlessly blending together to form such a magnificent structure.

He quietly opened the hatchway door and ventured out onto the roof to a beautiful dusk, taking care to keep low lest someone catch sight of him from below. The sun's deadly rays were gone, but he dare not become careless and give away his trusted sanctuary. A quick scan displayed the Evergreen Cemetery as John could never have imagined it.

Monuments, graves, and mausoleums dotted the grounds as he looked to the south and west. It was not only that the Gatehouse had been respectfully cared for; the cemetery landscaping was also in excellent condition. The people of Gettysburg were evidently proud of Evergreen, and it showed in the meticulous care, almost like a show of love.

But he was not alone. He heard two men talking just below him. John raised his head slowly above the brickwork to see and hear just what was going on at this hour.

"I'm sorry, but I live in the Gatehouse, so I really don't like people walking through the building. You see, as the caretaker, I am allowed that as part of my arrangement with the Association."

"Of course, I understand. Could you at least answer a couple of questions that I had about the interior of the building? I try to be as accurate as possible, even though it's a supernatural historical fiction story."

"I'm sorry, but I don't really approve of that type of subject matter for the Gatehouse, so I would have to say no to that also; nothing personal, you understand."

John wondered just how many caretakers there had been since Peter Thorn and his wife Elizabeth had tended to the cemetery's needs. In fact, the history of Evergreen itself might make for interesting reading. There certainly must be enough subject matter available for such a book if someone were to assume the undertaking.

The caretaker walked back into the building while the disappointed stranger got into his car and drove back out onto the Baltimore Pike. There was no one else in sight, a perfect opportunity for John to leave his perch and start another evening of curious investigation. A quick jump up and over the edge landed John near the roadway that snaked under the arches of the building.

It looked as good as any place to start, so he followed it until he came to a tall granite obelisk with the profile of a man on it surrounded by scrollwork. John glanced down at the inscription near the base. It read: General James Gettys—Proprietor of Gettysburg. So he had stumbled upon the grave of the founder himself. He wondered what the brave patriot who had fought in two wars for his country would think of his town today.

As he walked further up the path he noticed several people standing by a grave with a flagpole displaying a flag of the

United States at its top. John thought that perhaps it was another person of some importance, so he made the decision to check further.

It was the same old couple that he had met at the Jennie Wade Museum. The woman was talking a blue streak, but surprisingly, this time her husband was in complete agreement with her.

"That Cyclorama painting was the most inspiring sight that I have ever seen on canvas, Tom. The images were breathtaking, the colors so vivid, and the faces so lifelike that I felt for a moment that I was actually right in the middle of Picket's Charge."

"Anne, I couldn't agree with you more. Come to think of it, I can't remember the last time I agreed with you on anything, so the painting HAD to be good. I honestly don't believe our trip to Gettysburg would have been complete without it."

John came up casually from behind them. "Excuse me, I couldn't help but overhear you talking about this…Cyclorama painting. Could you tell me where I might find it?"

The old man turned to answer. "It's at the new Visitor's Center just down the road, but don't forget to bring your wallet. They charge for everything…I take that back. The bathrooms are still free, but they might start charging for use of the toilet stalls any day now if their revenues don't improve."

His wife replied swiftly; "Oh, Tom; that's not nice to say…even if it is true. You'll love the painting, young man. Is this your first time in Gettysburg?"

"I just arrived back here after a long absence, so I'm sort of feeling my way around again."

"Well, good luck to you, and enjoy the rest of your stay." She took her husband by the arm. "Come on, Tom, it is getting dark. If we get back to the Colton right away we still might be able to watch Jeopardy."

"God forbid you miss seeing Alex Trebek for one night, Anne. YOU watch Jeopardy. I'll take a shower and exfoliate with one of those luxurious bath towels. I just hope my skin doesn't peel off."

John smiled and watched with amusement as the couple walked away, but the smile vanished when he glanced back to the grave they were visiting. It was his Jennie's!

A statue of a woman stood atop the large monument in a flowing dress with a forlorn look on her face. Jennie's name was etched in twice, but at the bottom a large bronze plate was attached to the base, almost as an afterthought. It read MARY VIRGINIA WADE, her real name, in large capital letters.

John though fate especially cruel to have guided him to the one grave in the cemetery that he had not the slightest desire to see, but then again he was beginning to get used to fate acting in that manner, at least towards him. He decided to cut short his tour and go to the Visitor's Center before it closed. He had no idea when closing time might be, but he wanted to see that painting the old couple spoke of very badly. The full cemetery excursion would have to wait for another time.

John cut a wide turn to the left and noticed yet another flagpole. As there were no others in the area that he could see besides Jennie's, he was drawn towards it. He was not disappointed this time.

The grave belonged to none other than John Burns, the old Gettysburg resident who had inspired the young boys and girls of the town with his stories about the War of 1812. One word was etched proudly on the base of the grave; it read simply PATRIOT.

John thought that to be a fitting tribute. He remembered Burns as a scruffy old soul who was prone to being cranky at times, but he always secretly admired him for his service to his country. It was wonderful that he had not been forgotten in death.

That thought made John pause for a moment. He had not bumped into his tormentor/guardian angel Death the previous evening, not that he was complaining. He WAS surprised though, given their past history.

He finally made it back to the Cemetery Gatehouse and passed under the arches, giving the bricks a pat with his hand as he went toward the Baltimore Pike. A right turn put him on his way to the Visitor's Center, and he quickened his pace as he was unsure just how far he needed to go. Cars passed him by without so much as a look from the passengers inside, that is, until a large white car with a red, white, and blue attachment on its top slowly pulled up.

The driver gave him an ominous look, and when the car passed, he read the words Gettysburg Police on the side doors. John suddenly had a feeling of alarm but did not know why. He knew that he was breaking no laws. But that did not prevent the police car from coming to a stop further up the road.

To his surprise, when John reached it, the passenger door window moved downward and disappeared completely as if by magic, and a man in a blue uniform bent over slightly to make eye contact with him before he spoke.

"Nice night for a walk. Where you headed tonight, pal?"

John knew that this could be trouble if he did not satisfy the man's curiosity. "I'm headed over to the Visitor's Center to view the Cyclorama Painting. I want to make sure I get there before the place closes."

The officer dropped his guard a bit. "OK, I can go along with that, but the Center closes in about an hour. Why don't you hop in and I'll give you a ride?"

"Thanks, I think I'll take you up on that."

John felt that the officer was being kind only to question him further, but he also knew it would have aroused more suspicion if he declined the favor. He made a move for the front side door, but the officer pointed him to the back. John pulled up on the handle and the door swung open. As he sat down and closed the door behind him he realized several things, none of which inspired confidence.

For starters, there was wire mesh above the front seat that effectively imprisoned him in the rear portion of the car. Second, there were no handles on the back doors to allow him to get out on his own, and once the back door closed he began to smell the scent of rotting meat. This could only mean one thing; the police officer was a Freemason!

But the biggest problem he faced was staring right in front of him in the form of the rear view mirror, which was slowly beginning to crack. As a night creature, he cast no reflection, which affected the integrity of the mirror itself. If the officer decided to make use of it to check him out further during the ride, then all could be lost.

John began to retch. He needed to control himself and stomach the smell until they reached the Visitor's Center, or else he might have to smash through one of the windows and take to the sky for safety. A move like that would ruin his disguise and alert every Freemason in the area. He assumed the order still existed. The question was: how strong were their numbers?

The patrol car picked up speed as John attempted to get comfortable. "So why isn't a fella like you driving around instead of hoofing it from place to place?"

John reverted back to an old rule and attempted to mix truth in with his lies; that made it all easier to remember at a later date if need be. "I really don't think I have enough money to own a car right now; perhaps at some later date." He gaged but kept the sound down to a minimum, cupping his mouth with his right hand.

John unwittingly hit the right spot, and the officer softened. "I can understand where you're coming from on that end."

My brother and I had to share a car when we were teenagers growing up. Boy, did we have some fights over it come the weekends. My dad said he felt more like a referee than a father sometimes."

Fortunately, the Visitor's Center was much closer than John could ever have hoped for. As he began to gag all the harder, the patrol car slowed down and made a turn past a grey stone wall with an attached redwood sign that spelled out:

Gettysburg National Military Park Visitors Center

A short winding drive led them directly to a parking lot with a large information kiosk adjacent to it at the start of the main pathway. The car came to a stop as the officer got out and opened the back door for his reluctant rider. John exited the car and took in a deep breath of fresh air, but his expression gave him away.

"You don't look too good, kid. Do you get carsick sitting in the back?"

"I guess you could say that, yes. I want to thank you for giving me a ride over here officer..."

"Ferguson...Jack Ferguson; no problem, kid. Enjoy the museum."

John tried his best not to look anxious as he turned and began making his way up the slight incline to the Visitors Center. He could still feel the officer's eyes on him as he made a conscious effort to control his feet from walking too fast.

Finally, when he reached the Lincoln statue, he felt safe. Ferguson got back into his patrol car, turned back for one last look, and drove off onto the exit road.

John speculated as to how he would gain admission to this building. There were no people out front or in the lobby for that matter to help him garner an invitation. But that dilemma was immediately addressed. As he got to the entrance door, he noticed a small sign on the glass facing; it simply read: WEL-COME.

That was all he needed; he pushed on the door handle and walked into the lobby. Along a side wall he saw a long ticket booth staffed by several women wearing red polo shirts, much like the ones he swapped his clothes for at the Great T Shirt Company. He walked up to one of them and cleared his throat before speaking.

"I'd like to purchase a ticket for the Cyclorama Painting, please."

"I can help you with that, sir. The price is $10.50, but that includes the movie A New Birth of Freedom if you're interested."

"No thank you; just the painting." He handed over a $20.00 bill and received a ticket and change, after which he was directed to what appeared to be a stairway, but the stairs were moving! He placed one foot on it and began to slide forward, losing his balance in the process. Two teenagers behind him started to laugh, and then one of them spoke up.

"Hey, dude, are you Polish or drunk? Try both feet."

John followed the instructions without a reply or look back and the escalator carried him to the second floor. He chose the stairs for his ascension to the actual Cyclorama Painting. The circular room was dark. He could make out a continuous battle scene lining the walls as he worked his way around the carpeted platform.

A tall, attractive young woman who John assumed to be the speaker waited for people to work their way up to and around her. She was dressed much like the sales clerks behind the downstairs ticket counter. When it appeared that there were no more stragglers, she picked up a black rod and began speaking into it. Somehow her voice seemed to explode around the room from every direction.

"Good evening everyone, I'm Jennifer Brown, and welcome to the Companions of Gettysburg's restoration of Paul Philippoteaux's The Battle of Gettysburg Cyclorama. The actual cost of the restorative work was close to $16 million dollars, and the painting was re-opened for public viewing in 2008 here at the Visitors Center." The people began to crowd around her as she spoke.

"The Battle of Gettysburg Cyclorama is a depiction of the famous attack that we today refer to as Pickett's Charge; that moment in July of 1863, when 12,000 Confederates attacked and reached the Union lines positioned at Cemetery Ridge. Many historians believe it was after this charge that the South began its slow decline into eventual defeat two years later in 1865.

This painting gives us a unique perspective in that it shows how events would have been seen in the center of the Union lines on the crest of the ridge. If you look closely, you will recognize many of the important military figures from both sides.

The artist has drawn them performing their actual feats of heroism from that fateful day. I will now begin the recorded portion of the presentation, and will be happy to answer any questions you may have upon its conclusion."

Lights flashed, the sounds of battle echoed through the room, and a deep voiced narrator gave a step by step explanation of the events from the High Water Mark of the Confederacy. John glanced down and saw various battlefield implements strategically placed all around the base of the painting to stimulate the illusion of the viewer actually standing behind the lines during that exact moment in American history.

No one was more impressed than John, for he remembered walking that same hallowed ground on the night of July 3rd in 1863. Everything was present in the painting except for the moans of the dying and the terrible stench of death. This Philippoteaux fellow had certainly captured the battle on an elemental level. John lowered his head and closed his eyes as he recalled the bloated, ravaged remains of what were once brave men.

"Are you all right? People usually don't react like this to the Cyclorama as much as you have. Do you have a family member hidden somewhere here in the painting from way back?" Someone was hovering over John in his reverie. He opened his eyes to see the young woman who had given the presentation.

"You could say something like that, yes. I guess I kind of got caught up in the moment. Thank you for the show. It was very informative."

The crowd began to exit the room. "You're welcome; it's good to see someone become so connected to the painting. That's exactly how I felt the first time I saw it. A bunch of us volunteered to prep it for just what you see now. I loved every minute of it…Are you here visiting Gettysburg and the battlefield?

"Yes, you could say that."

"Well…maybe I'll see you around. I'm a Gettysburg resident. My name's Jen Brown, but you already know that from my intro, don't you?"

"John Larson…it's nice to meet you, Jen, and thanks again."

He followed the last of the Cyclorama patrons out of the room and down to the lobby area as the Visitors Center readied to close for the evening. John thought about her on the way. This was the first time that he could remember a girl showing any interest in him. Unfortunately, it no longer mattered.

CHAPTER 18

Of Mines and Monuments

"Hey Luther, pass me one of them Slim Jims in the glove compartment, will ya? I'm pretty sure there's a few left."

"And I'm pretty sure you need to keep your mind on your fuckin' job, Jasper. Hold those tanks close together back there. I don't want to hear any of them clanking around, you understand?"

"All right, all right, no need to get your balls all twisted. It'd be helpful if you drove a mite slower around the turns. Remember, you got no seats in the back of this van."

Luther drove around the traffic circle and up Baltimore Street past the courthouse and library. When he passed the Shriver House Museum he slowed down as a police car was entering from South Street.

"Shit! Can you believe this luck? I'm driving right behind a goddamn cop."

"Better in back than in front...and don't get too close, Luther. You tailgate like a motherfucker."

"One more word out of you and I'll throw the Slim Jims out the window, and you know I'll do it."

The rest of the drive was in silence. Luther Stokes was contemplating the placement of his IED's, and Jasper Fields thought of his Slim Jims as his stomach growled in anger. They continued onto the Baltimore Pike past the Visitors Center, over Route 15, to The Outlet Shoppes at Gettysburg. It was a veritable shopaholic's delight, with a large parking area that was perfect to avoid detection. The van circled for a space and eventually parked in the vicinity of TGI Fridays.

"Hey Luther, why didn't we just park the van at the Visitor's Center? We got at least a good 10 to 15 minute walk ahead of us now."

"The Visitors Center's closed now, dickhead. If we were to park in the lot, it would be a tipoff that someone was prowling the grounds after hours. The stores here close soon too, but Fridays is open until 1AM. Any security staff driving around will think we're just hanging out there.

Now load up the stuff—two propane tanks for each duffle bag, and watch how you put them in. I don't want the boxes of screws to come loose; remember they're only held to the outside of the tanks by duct tape. I'll handle the rest of the equipment."

"Hot damn but you sure got everything figured out real good, Luther. What's our next step?"

"Hand me one of the bags. I'll go out first and head for the woods. After five minutes, you do the same and follow me. I'll be waiting for you and then we'll hike over together."

"We gotta walk through the WOODS? We can walk along the Pike and get there a hell of a lot quicker."

"That's right, and we can also be spotted by every asshole that drives by, including the police. You really have to start using your head, Jasper. I'm going out now; when you see me reach the woods, wait the five minutes and come out towards me, got it?"

"Got it, Luther; you can count on me."

"We'll see about that, too." Stokes opened the driver side door and got out, slinging the duffle bag over his right shoulder while holding a small knapsack in his left hand. He made a bee line for the woods and disappeared into the brush while the parking lot was clear of people.

Jasper watched him intently and moved to the front of the van with his own duffle, sitting down in the passenger seat. While he was well into his count, he remembered the Slim Jims and opened the glove compartment for a snack, but they were gone. After the five minutes were up, Jasper followed his instructions. The two men were reunited and on their way to the Visitors Center.

"Damn, Luther, you ate the rest of the Slim Jims didn't you?"

"Ate them up last night and shit them out this morning, my friend. Now we're going to go single file with you right behind me. Be sure to step where I step. I don't want any broken ankles before we get there."

"What about on the way back?"

"If I break an ankle on the way back, you help me to the van. If you break an ankle, I slit your throat and leave you in the woods."

"I know you're only saying that so's I concentrate on my steppin' Luther, right?"

"Yeah, right; here we go. Keep two or three paces behind me at the most."

The pair snaked their way carefully through the woods until they came to Route 15, where they stopped out of sight just short of the roadbed shoulder. "All right, Jasper, we'll wait until the next car passes. I don't see any headlights coming in either direction after that. We'll do this together, understand?"

"You got it, Luther; just say the word."

"Aaaand Nowwww!" The men scampered out of the shadows.

"Jesus, Luther, now I know what a raccoon feels like when he's crossin' the road."

"Route 15 means that we're halfway there. It won't be long now." And it wasn't; in another quarter hour they reached the back of the Visitor's Center.

"Listen, this is how we get to the spot I picked out. We hug the walls low and slow without a sound, not even so much as a fart, you understand, Jasper?"

"Wh…whatever you say…L..Luther."

"Don't punk out on me now, boy. If you want to get anywhere in the Priesthood, you need to buck up and pull your weight, got it?"

"I got it…I got it! Let's get this show on the road."

Another 10 minutes of crawling in the grass placed them at the mother lode, the long row of spreading emerald green arborvitae in the immediate vicinity of the Lincoln statue. The two men sat up against the wall of the building with the shrubs in front of them as their cover. Both took a deep breath of relief for a moment.

"So far so good, Jasper; the worst is over. No one can see us in this dead spot. We can pretty much do whatever we please now, so let's concentrate on placing the tanks. Put yours down behind the second and third shrubs; I'll put mine down behind the sixth and seventh. That will give us a pretty wide swathe once they blow up. Boy, the green spray paint really blends the tanks in with the shrubs. No one will be able to detect them."

"We wanna get as many of those boogies as we can, huh, Luther?"

"Absolutely, and whoever we don't kill with the blasts will still get pretty fucked up from the screws, plus we do serious damage to the building. Now...just let me hook the wiring and charges to each of the valve stems...then attach the transceiver and cellphone...THERE! We're set to go.

All that we need to do now is wait for the festivities at the statue tomorrow night. When you give me the signal, I'll make the call, and Mr. Lincoln's statue will think the Civil War has started up again."

"That's real funny, Luther. No wonder August likes you so much. Can we go back now?"

"Yeah; you did OK so far, my friend, but tomorrow's the real test. You think you got it in you?"

"Why...why sure, Luther; like I said before, you can count on me. Th..That's the honest truth...so help me God."

"You'll need help from God if you do anything to fuck up this operation. All right, we'll work our way back to the van the same way we got here. Follow me, and keep your smelly ass down. I'm sure that with a place like this, security's got to be making rounds at some point in the evening. We're too close to success to be seen now by some rent a cop or park flunky."

While Luther Stokes and Jasper Fields were making their way back to safety, John Larson was reveling in his time in the air. After so many years of imprisonment, he had made it a point not to recall the sheer enjoyment of flight.

There was too much freedom involved in such thoughts. Something like that would surely have driven him mad, as the

Vampire Council had cruelly predicted. It was one of his many safeguards to insure his sanity, and it paid off.

John's sky journey eventually took him over the darkness of the battlefield. From his eagle's view he could just make out dozens of monuments with vague shapes and sizes. The late hour of the evening would cancel out the prospect of an accidental encounter. He had heard of the park curfew, or closing hours as they were called now, while he was at the Visitors Center, and he was also aware of the staffers who drove around to ensure that "vandalism" was reduced.

He was, however, clueless as to what the term vandalism referred to, although it did sound like the hordes of Germanic tribes that invaded Italy in the 5th century and laid waste to mighty Rome. He remembered that much from his classical history while at the Agricultural College.

John was drawn to a light on the darkened fields below around Oak Hill. As he grew closer he saw that it was a gas flame in a large bronze urn sitting on top of a square limestone shaft that was close to 40 feet high. It rose from the middle of a long granite platform. There were stairs on either end so people could walk about.

On the front of the shaft was a bas relief consisting of two women walking together in lockstep; one was holding a wreath, and the other a shield while a proud eagle led them forward. John felt that it must have been meant as a sign of unity between North and South. On the opposite side of the shaft were the words: With Firmness In The Right As God Gives Us To See The Right—-Lincoln.

The night creature was moved. Even though his metamorphosis had greatly diminished his emotions, his "passion," that one last vestige of untouched humanity, was still his patriotism. He wished he had been present at the dedication of this monument, and then it struck him that he WAS on the battlefield when it took place, but he was interred, devoid of all outside contact.

This was truly an impressive structure, and John was pleased that words spoken by Mr. Lincoln were included, as he would have been the first to approve of such a monument. That quote was also a reminder. He knew that the North had prevailed in its mission to preserve the Union and end slavery, but how did the President rally the country after the war's end?

He wanted desperately to find out, but this was not the time or the place. Perhaps tomorrow night he would make it a point to find the answer; for the rest of the evening, what little there was left, he would try to discover one more, grand memorial. He thought about suitable locations on the battlefield, and he immediately remembered Pickett's Charge in the Cyclorama Painting.

If there was another monument of great importance, it would be somewhere along the Emmitsburg Road in the place that he had walked one evening so many years ago. He took to the air once again. In a short time he was over the quiet fields that sucked up so much blood on the last day of the battle, and there in all its magnificence was a sight so beautiful it nearly took his breath away.

His eyes were immediately drawn to a white granite dome with a bronze woman standing in its center. She held a sword in one hand and a palm leaf in the other in an obvious attempt to present both victory and peace. She was at least 100 feet high.

This dome was supported by four large granite archways, with eight bronze statues of military and political figures from the war set in on their sides. Above them were battle scene monoliths.

The rectangular granite base was lined with bronze tablets, as were the inside walls. They listed the names of all the units and Pennsylvania boys who fought at Gettysburg. John made it a point to walk around the monument to take in all of its grandeur.

While doing so he read the inscriptions under the statues. It was a who's who of Keystone State dignitaries: George Meade, John Reynolds, Winfield Scott Hancock, David Birney, Alfred Pleasanton, and David Gregg.

He recognized a few of the names, but not all. He assumed the rest were Union military figures who distinguished themselves in the war. However, he did not need to read the inscriptions of the last two figures to know who they were, President Abraham Lincoln and Pennsylvania Governor Andrew Curtin.

They were in his conscious memory when he made the fateful trip to Etenel Babako, just before the damned war broke out. Within the monument was a staircase that led to the roof for a panoramic view of the surrounding area, but that was unnecessary for a night creature.

The monument text was direct and to the point; it read: *The Commonwealth of Pennsylvania in honor of her sons who on this field fought for the Preservation of the Union— July 1, 2, 3, 1863.* He wondered about the cost of such a structure, and how it was paid for. In a way, he wished he had been present for the fundraising. He would have been proud to contribute any money he had as a way to thank those who served.

Just then lights began to weave their way toward him from the direction of the Peach Orchard. From the configuration and their intensity he knew that it was an automobile of some sort, most probably a park guard ensuring that no one was on the grounds after closing time.

As the truck drove slowly past him, he hid behind the staircase until the coast was clear, and then decided to call it a night. The clueless driver was quite fortunate. John was beginning to feel hungry.

He took to the sky and was soon near the intersection of Steinwehr Avenue and the Taneytown Road, making a sweep towards his sweet refuge atop the Cemetery Gatehouse when he detected the faint whiff of rotting meat below. Could that man

Ferguson have recognized him for what he truly was and stirred up his fellow Freemasons?

Were they closing in on his resting place at this very moment? Perhaps the policeman had not been as stupid as he appeared. He detected no movement from below, but the smell continued, so he took the risk and swooped down into what he thought to be that National Cemetery he had heard about.

A brief reconnoiter brought him face to face with a grim sight. There not 10 feet in front of him was a small but distinctive monument. Two soldiers were on a granite slab; one was on his knees tending to an injured comrade prostrate on his back.

The gold etching on the face of the memorial's base read: Friend to Friend—A Brotherhood Undivided. However, that was not the problem. Also shown was the well-known Masonic intersecting square and compass, with a large G in its center. He didn't know who was depicted in the scene, but that was irrelevant.

John's enemies were not only still present in and around Gettysburg, but they were thriving…like rats during the Black Plague. Even without a single Freemason in sight he could still smell their stench around this tribute to their cursed brotherhood. He needed more information if he was to stay out of danger.

CHAPTER 19

A Change In Plans

"Can I take you out for some breakfast, darlin'? It's the least I can do."

"I think I'll take you up on that. By the way, in case you forgot, my name's Charlene."

Luther Stokes massaged his temples slowly with his hands in an effort to wipe away the cobwebs, but to no avail. "Of course I remember your name...Charlene. How could I forget the name of such a sweet thing like you?"

"Very easily, considering all the beer you drank last night at the Blue Parrott. By the way, what happened to your friend?"

"Oh, you mean Jasper. Well, he and I had kind of like an agreement...of sorts."

"Let me guess; the agreement was whoever got lucky would get the hotel room."

"Ahhh, yeah, that's about it, honey. He's probably still asleep in his pickup truck."

"Well, why don't you see how he's doing while I take a shower? I think you owe HIM a breakfast too."

"That may make him a little less ornery today, that's for sure." Luther put on his shirt and pants and left the hotel room sans footwear. His gait was a bit unsteady; fortunately, the room was on the ground floor, so he didn't have to navigate stairs, and it led directly to the parking lot. He struggled towards a pickup truck that had seen better days. Sitting in the driver's seat was a miserable looking Jasper Fields.

"Hey, there, Jasper; we're headed out to breakfast in a bit and thought you might like to..."

"Don't try to be nice to me, Luther, it's not like you. While you were getting' yours and then sleeping in the air conditioning, I was stuck out here in this goddamn heat...was up most of the night, too."

"I know, I know, but she was too good to pass up. Anyway, why don't you come with us? You've got to be hungry."

"Just get her the hell out of here. I'm goin' back to the room in 10 minutes to get some sleep and a.c."

"OK, Jasper, I'll bring you back something from the diner."

Luther Stokes had plenty to feel good about as he walked back to the room—the explosives were in place, set to blow on his signal, AND he had just gotten laid. The only potential problem was directly overhead. The sky was dark for 9AM. It looked like a nasty storm was set to dump some rain on his parade. What he needed was a weather report, and fast.

When he got back to the room Charlene emerged from the bathroom and gave him a big kiss while wrapping her arms around his neck. "How is your friend doing?"

"As well as can be expected; let's get a move on. I'm getting hungry." The couple exited the Super 8 and walked to Luther's van, then they made the short trip along York Street and past Baltimore Street, parking in front of the Avenue Restaurant. The diner had a fine view for people watching from its picture window fronting Steinwehr Avenue, and the two made good use of it as they sat down.

"So you guys are here on your own little Civil War trip. How long do you expect to be here in Gettysburg?"

"Just another day or so; it depends on how much we can see."

"Well, you're not going to see much today. It's started to rain, and I believe it's going to get heavy and go through the night; lots of storm warnings. It came in suddenly from Canada."

Luther became agitated at this turn of events. "What are you, some kind of weather junkie?"

"Sort of; I was going to go into meteorology at college, but I got bored after a couple of semesters and dropped out. I work at the National Military Store on Taneytown Road...but it's only temporary, you understand. I'm going to get it together soon enough and decide what it is I want to do."

Luther pretended to show an interest, but he had to get information quickly on the midnight event to see if it had been cancelled.

"Sure; take your time. There's no need to make any rash decisions." A painfully slow 30 minutes later, the two had finished breakfast.

"Can I ask you a question, Luther?"

"Sure, go right ahead."

"Why do you have a swastika on your arm?"

Stokes was taken back. "How do you know that?"

"When you were asleep I noticed it under the covers. What are you, some kind of terrorist or something?"

He forced a short laugh and smiled pleasantly. "That's something I got a while back when I was drunk one night. My friends had it put there as a joke. I've been meaning to have it removed, but just never got around to it."

"Well, that makes me feel better. And there was another tattoo below it, a capital letter P with a horizontal line through its center."

"That's...for my mom...Patricia."

"Good; for a minute there I thought you were one of those Tim McVeigh types...you know, that Oklahoma City bombing guy."

"Ohhh, right; I remember him now...pretty shitty business back then with all those people blown to bits and all. I'm glad they executed him."

Luther knew that if his plans played out as expected, Charlene would be quickly reminded of the stranger she slept with the night before the explosions, the one with the strange tattoos.

"Charlene, what do you say you take me for a ride around and show me the sights?"

"I don't see why not. It's Saturday, and I've got the whole weekend off."

"Great...why don't we get started? My chariot awaits." Luther mustered up some dark thoughts. The nosy bitch would have to die, and her body had to remain undetected until after he and Jasper left town. He counted on her taking him for a guided tour of the countryside. A quiet secluded spot would do nicely; that would prove no problem with the rain increasing.

The best that he could do for Charlene was kill her quickly, which he did, but only after they had another romp in his van. He found the unique situation of having sex with a woman before murdering her strangely exhilarating. An hour later he

185

was walking up the main walkway to the Visitors Center in a driving rain.

A casual glance at the arborvitae along the side of the building by the Lincoln statue showed not the slightest hint of detection towards his IEDs. While the heavy rain might possibly change the celebration timetable of Company F, it was also a good thing in that there would be less chance of some landscaper stumbling upon the makeshift bombs.

He made his way through the entrance doors, fluffed up his clear plastic parka to rid himself of excess rain, and went straight to the information booth in the lobby. The three women behind the counter flocked to him out of boredom. The Center was nearly empty due to the inclement weather.

"Excuse, me ladies, but I wonder if you might be able to help me. I know that Company F of the United States Colored Troops was to have a ceremony here tonight at midnight. I had planned on attending it, but I wanted to make sure that it was still scheduled for this evening."

One woman piped up quickly. "Oh, no, the weather report has scotched that plan. It has been re-scheduled as a beautiful dawn ceremony tomorrow morning. The rain's supposed to leave the area around 2 or 3AM and then clear up nicely…but that's not the REAL news."

"Oh, what could be better than that?"

"Well, I heard it from my friend in the Bookstore, who overheard it from someone in the National Park Service main office, that there was going to be a special surprise guest, a real VIP, not just some guy from the Department of the Interior."

Luther's antennae went up. "But you don't know who this person is?"

"Nope; it's a big secret. No one can seem to find out who it is."

One of the other women chimed in. "Maybe the Vice President's coming!"

The youngest of the three made a face and sounded disappointed. "That WOULD be a surprise, but it wouldn't be special. Joe Biden's scary stupid. That a-hole couldn't strangle a giraffe."

While the ladies began to argue politics amongst themselves, Luther turned around and put up a goodbye wave as he exited the Center, casting one last glance over to the arborvitae and giving them a wink for luck. When he reached the parking lot, he got into his van and made a hurried call on his cell phone.

"Hello August? It's me, Luther."

"I was just about to call you, Luther. I have some VERY good news for you."

"Really? What is it?"

"You were probably calling to tell me that there's a surprise guest coming to the ceremony."

"That's right! How did you know?"

"Forget about that. The rain delay has freed up the schedule of someone who is very high on our list, Luther...right up there at the top of the heap."

"Who? Come on, August, don't break my balls. Tell me!"

"Are you ready? Colin Fucking Powell, my man; this is like a gift from heaven."

"It almost sounds too good to be true, August. This is going to be fantastic!"

"You're spot dead on, Luther. Powell's the second most dangerous one of the group, behind that mulatto bastard in the White House. There's nothing worse than a nigger who can act and talk like a white man. That's what gets people to vote for them or worse, put them in high positions in our military."

"Right; I just got back from the Visitors Center, August. Nothing has been disturbed and we'll be ready to go first thing tomorrow at dawn. Do you think they'll be extra security now because of Powell?"

"My sources have heard just a couple of suits for show, nothing more. He's no longer in politics, and he's retired from the Army. Besides, it's supposed to be a surprise."

"Oh, it'll be a surprise all right. Hey Luther, I had a bit of a problem here, but I got it straightened out.

"What kind of problem?"

"I had to off someone who could have been a potential problem. The body's been stashed in the woods, covered in burlap and bungees. No one will find it for a while...I promise."

"That's why I chose you for this mission, Luther, to take care of emergencies as they arise. Good work. Be sure to keep an eye on Jasper, know what I mean?"

"I do; he won't be a problem, but if he is, I'll handle it like I always do."

"Great; good luck tomorrow. It looks as though the weather should break for you just in time. Call me when you're on the way home. Let us pray for success. Goodbye, Luther."

Stokes climbed into the van and made his way back to the Super 8 Motel. When he unlocked the door to the room, Jasper Fields was watching Conan the Barbarian on channel 56. He looked about as good as Jasper Fields could, which was passable at best, even for a redneck.

"Jasper, wait till you hear the news."

"Hold it a second, Luther. My favorite line from the whole movie is coming up." Arnold Schwarzenegger was dressed in a loincloth sitting around with some Mongols when the leader asked one of his generals a philosophical question, at least for a Mongol.

"What is best in life?"

"The open steppe, a fleet horse, falcons at your wrist, the wind in your hair."

"WRONG! Conan, what is best in life?"

"Crush your enemies, see them driven in chains before you, exalt in the lamentation of their women."

"That is good! That is good!"

"God I love that Conan...What's up, Luther? How'd it go with that girl last night? She sure was a pretty thing; you get any?"

"Yeah, but she was a dead lay. I have some great news. Colin Powell will be at the ceremony tomorrow morning. We're going to hit the jackpot, my friend."

Jasper's eyes widened in fear; "Hot damn, Luther. That's a game changer...a big deal...a very big deal."

"Meaning what?" Stokes moved menacingly towards his now reluctant cohort. "Remember what I said I'd do to you in the woods?"

Jasper put up his hands with his palms out. "I'm cool, Luther; really I am. Relax, will ya? I just gotta get used to the news, that's all."

"Fine, because you're in all the way on this one, Jasper. There's no backing out at this point. Now I'm going out to McDonald's to pick up some lunch and dinner, then gas up the van. How's your pickup truck for gas?"

"I still got three quarters of a tank."

"Fine; you stay the fuck right here and don't move. We're going to sit tight in the room until tomorrow morning's ceremony."

"But you said I could have another go at that monument. It's raining heavy and there won't be anyone around for sure to catch me in the act."

"FORGET the fucking monument. We've got bigger fish to fry. I'm heading out now. You want anything special from Mickey D's, like a Happy Meal and a vanilla shake?"

"Very funny," Jasper said dejectedly. "I'll have whatever you get. Are you stoppin' off for some beer to wash it down with?"

"No, you ass wipe; we need clear heads in the morning. You'll take a Pepsi and like it."

As Luther shut the door behind him, Jasper cursed under his breath. "FUCK YOU, Luther. I'm STILL doin' it."

CHAPTER 20

Wine And Spirits

John awoke in his attic crawlspace to the sound of a pelting rain on the roof of the Cemetery Gatehouse. He had not felt rain on his face for well over a century, and he actually looked forward to it again, but not with such intensity. He knew that if he continued his night tour of the new Gettysburg, he would get totally drenched without some kind of foul weather gear.

Unfortunately, the clothing that he previously bartered for at the Great T Shirt Company did not include such items, but he hoped he could rustle something up among the boxes, bags and crates in his sanctuary. John had made no previous attempts to discover just what things were being sequestered around him.

Their use as cover was all the information he needed at the time, but now, he began looking for a proper fitting raincoat. His initial search proved to be fruitless, and also bizarre. One box was filled with tequila flavored worm lollipops, while another contained a hookah. A nearby crate had a smiling sundial mixed in with several bowling pins marked 200 Game, while a white plastic bag hid a cheeseburger telephone with Jimmy Buffett's picture on the top of the bun.

None of this made any sense whatsoever to John, particularly the crash dummy sitting comfortably on a stack of books

191

in a far corner. He stopped for a moment and looked more closely around the attic. If the rest of his finds proved as strange, he would have to admit defeat and risk a serious soaking. Just then, on the floor covered partially in dust, was the item he was after.

John crept lightly towards it so as not to make any sound of footsteps to those below. He took it and headed back to the crawlspace door, opening it up and quickly popping open the umbrella to avoid the rain. As he clumsily worked his way onto the roof, he noticed that it was navy blue and white, with the words LOS ANGELES RAMS emblazoned on the canopy.

He was suddenly very happy to be out of that crawlspace chocked full of things beyond his comprehension. If it contained items that were indicative of what he needed to find out about the 21st century, then he had many months of catching up to do.

John briefly closed the umbrella and vaulted over the roof to the ground below, then re-opened it and began his walk along the Baltimore Pike. He had covered Steinwehr Avenue and Baltimore Street enough for him to desire another venue, and he could think of no better place than the Gettysburg's so called diamond, which he hoped was still there after all these years.

The rain temporarily held foot traffic to a minimum, even for a Saturday night. He passed few people on his way to the center of town. Finally, he arrived at his desired location, and he could think of no better place to investigate than the establishment that was staring him right in the face, the Pub and Restaurant, on the corner in Lincoln Square.

The building appeared to have previously been a private house. It was quite beautiful, with light colored stucco trimmed with dark blue window frames, shutters, canopies, and even its roofing. Tall green shrubs in whiskey barrels dotted the sidewalks, while hanging planters under the second floor windows were overflowing with a variety of colored flowers, giving off a pleasant vibe.

Yes, John wanted to visit this place, and he saw his opportunity standing right in the open doorway. A perky young hostess was standing just inside with a short stack of menus in her hand. He walked up and smiled, and she responded in kind.

"Hello, welcome to the Pub and Restaurant; are you here for drinks or dinner?"

"Ahhh, drinks only for now."

"Great! Come on in out of the rain and find a spot at the bar; it's on your left."

John complied and just like that he was inside, trying to get the bartender's attention for a beer. He had begun to find great amusement in the entrance restriction that had hampered so many of his kind in the past. In fact, he now considered himself somewhat of an expert in the subtle art of gaining interior access whenever necessary. Dumaine would have been thoroughly impressed.

The atmosphere of the interior decor tended towards a Victorian style, and even included tin ceilings, so John felt quite comfortable, except for the flat screen TV suspended overhead for the bar customers. A baseball game between the Phillies and Nationals was being televised without sound, not that it would have mattered. The conversations of the patrons, coupled with blaring music that seemed to be coming from nowhere and everywhere, made any audio commentary impossible to hear, even for John.

He had just flagged down the bartender and was inquiring about the beers on tap when a female voice chimed in. "Hey John, would you be interested in sharing a pitcher of Grimsters?" He turned to see Jen Brown standing beside him, but she was not the same girl he had met the night before at the Cyclorama Painting.

She word a full length/half sleeve black velvet dress, with black satin ribbons intertwining the bodice, and frilly black lace scrollwork on the neckline. Her short brown hair was gone, covered over by a wig of long flowing black hair. John's jaw dropped upon seeing her, which resulted in a half smirk and a twinkle in her eye before she spoke.

"I have to admit, it IS quite a makeover, but it helps pay the bills."

John was almost at a loss for words. "You're Jen…the girl from the Visitor's Center. Why are you dressed like…THIS?"

"It's my costume for the séance."

"The séance?"

"Yes, over at the Farnsworth House Bookstore; the owners recently turned a portion of the bookstore into a Victorian séance room. It's really cool. I'm one of their mediums. We reproduce 19th century séances, much like the ones people back then used to try to communicate with their dead loved ones. In fact, I'm doing one in about an hour from now."

John smiled. "And have you had any supernatural experiences, at least that you know of?"

"Oh, no; it's just for fun, although someday I hope to get the attention of some dead soldier's spirit that's floating around the area. Thousands of men died violently and suddenly here, so I'm always crossing my fingers that someday I'll make actual contact with the supernatural."

"Well, you never know Jen. This might be your lucky night."

"So about the pitcher; are you interested?"

"That depends on what's in a…Grimsters."

"It's the specialty of the house—white wine, apple and orange juice, peach schnapps, and some kind of liqueur that I can't pronounce."

"It sounds interesting. I could go for some of that."

Jen motioned to a waitress for the pitcher and pointed to the seating area. "Great; let's get a table. The show's about to start."

"What show?

"Saturday night is comics night at the Pub and Restaurant. People get up on stage for about 10 to 15 minutes and do their routines. Some of them are actually pretty funny."

"What about the ones who aren't funny?"

"We boo the living shit out of them for annoying us and they never come back."

The couple found a table in the corner, and a waitress brought over the pitcher of Grimsters Brew and two wine glasses. John poured the sweet smelling concoction into his companion's glass and then did the same for himself.

"Say John, I have an idea. Why don't you sit in on the séance later? There's still one or two spots left open."

He raised his eyebrows. "That sounds interesting. I think I'll take you up on that."

"Great; it's just a short walk to the bookstore and…OK, the show's about to start."

The music stopped, then the bartender picked up the remote control and turned off the television. All that was left was the buzzing of the crowd. A well to do looking gentleman got up on a small, well lit stage in the back corner of the room and raised his hands for silence. He waited several seconds and the customers quieted down.

"Thank you, folks; as you know, tonight is the night we showcase local comedic talent. We've got quite a few performers slated for this evening, so without further delay, let's get started with one of our own, a Gettysburg resident, veterinarian, and wannabe comedian—Dr. Jamie Oradell. Give it up for Doctor Jamie!"

A handsome man of about 40 bounded onto the stage to polite applause and waved to the crowd. "Hello everyone; I'm really excited to be here in Gettysburg, and especially at the Pub and Restaurant. As some of you may know, I was originally from New York, and I just arrived back from there. I attended the funeral of a cousin, who died unexpectedly. His obituary was so beautiful that I clipped it from the New York Post, and I want to read it to you all now."

The crowd grew inquisitive, particularly John. He didn't have the slightest inkling as to how an obituary could make its way into a comedy act, but Jen did. She was already smiling.

"Doctor Jamie treated my cat Bo at the animal hospital last week. He tried this bit out on me in the examination room. Wait till you hear it." She looked at John attentively, studying his face. Doctor Jamie took a piece of paper out of his shirt pocket and cleared his throat before proceeding in a somber tone while Jen refilled their glasses.

"Brooklyn contractor Grossfacio Unscrupulata, 62, of 100 Grotto Blvd., Bay Ridge, died yesterday from injuries received in the collapse of a building he was inspecting prior to sale at a public auction." Jamie paused for effect.

"Born in Madonna on the Half Shell, Sicily, Unscrupulata was brought to this country by boat at the age of 11 by his parents, Regurgito and Nauseata Unscrupulata." A man at a nearby table scarfing nachos without the use of utensils coughed up a laugh.

"Prior to his untimely death, Unscrupulata was President of the Negligento Construction Company, which was founded by his late brother, Devio. Before his association with the Negligento Construction Company, Unscrupulata worked for the Perfumo Cesspool Cleaning and Catering Corporation.

He is survived by his grieving wife, Inconsolata; their sons, Retardo, Cretino, and Imbecillio; daughters Overia, Fallopia, and Clitoria; two sisters, Miss Hysteria Psychosi and Mrs. Mammeria Pendulosa; a brother, Prolifico Fornicato, and 14 nieces and nephews." Most of the crowd was now laughing loudly.

"Active many years in community affairs, Unscrupulata was a member of the Sons of Sicily Backstabbers Society, the Il Duce Bocci Club, Insanitario's Pizzeria Bowling team, and past President of the renowned Bay Ridge Pink Flamingo Lawn and Garden Association. Until recently, he appeared at local carnivals and night clubs performing a knife throwing act with his late business partner, Inadverto Castrata.

The Reverend Celibato Unfortunato of the Saint Bastardo Roman Catholic Church will offer a solemn high requiem Night at the Races game on Wednesday. Interment will be at the Arrivederci Roma Memorial Park. Funeral arrangements will be handled carefully by the Rigor-Mortiso Funeral Parlor.

In lieu of flowers, the family asks that donations be sent directly to the James Gandolfini Fan Club. Ladies and Gentlemen, thank you so much for your respectful attention during this reading. God bless you."

The crowd hooped, hollered, and clapped roundly for Dr. Jamie's first skit. He was well on his way to a successful night, and all but one person appeared to have a smile on his face—John. Quite the contrary, he seemed totally confused at the reception upon the conclusion of the comic's reading. Jen was laughing more at John's expression than at Dr. Jamie's routine.

He had to be honest with her. "I had no idea what he was saying up there half of the time. He certainly mentioned a lot of words with vowels at the end, and who is James Galdolfini?"

"You really don't have a clue, do you John? Have you been out of the country for a while?"

"Something like that."

"Well, finish your drink and let's get going. It'll take a few extra minutes for us to walk to the bookstore in this rain, and I need to get there early to soak in the mood. Wait until you see how the room is set up. It's fantastic."

The two exited and crossed the street when John got another whiff of rotting meat. He wondered if he was being followed, and his eyes shifted across the diamond to what looked like a small entrance door. "Jen, what's over there next to that dress store, near the statue of President Lincoln?"

"You mean the one with the man staring out from behind the front door? That's the Good Samaritan Temple, one of those weird Masonic Lodges. The members wear raccoon hats, dance the polka in women's clothing, and perform unspeakable human sacrifices."

John looked at her in amazement and started to laugh long and hard. He thought it felt good, despite his sudden proximity to danger. Was that man in the doorway waiting innocently for the rain to subside, or was it something more sinister?

"Well, Doctor Jamie didn't get you to laugh, but I did. That's a good sign, don't you think? We're simpatico."

She edged closer to him under his out of place LA Rams umbrella as they walked along. If this had been another time, John would have been ecstatic, but fate had deemed otherwise. He pretended to smile in agreement. He couldn't help but think what a wonderful girl she was.

The couple walked the rest of the way in silence as the rain drenched everything but the two of them. They finally arrived at the Farnsworth House and took the pathway on the left to the bookstore's entrance. A woman with a concerned look met them at the door.

"I'm so glad you made it without getting soaked Jen. That dress would have weighed a ton. Oh...and who's your handsome gentleman friend? Do come in."

"Be nice, Pat. John Larson, this is my friend AND boss, Pat O'Day, so be on your best behavior. She runs the bookstore, among lots of other good things. Pat, I invited John to join in the séance; that's OK isn't it?"

"That's perfect; we have one opening left, and the last person that's registered gets to sit on the right side of our medium. He can complete the circle this evening. Have you ever participated in a séance before, John?"

"No, this is my first one."

"Well, we hope to have an interesting evening of entertainment for you and your fellow guests. All right, everyone, if you would all step this way into the parlor, we can begin the séance."

John counted eight people for the séance, including Jen and himself. It was a hodgepodge group of spook seekers. Once again, John had found a way to bump into his senior citizen friends Tom and Anne, while a set of boy/girl twins around ten years old tiptoed wide eyed into the room, followed quickly by their watchful parents. The room was set for the festivities to begin.

CHAPTER 21

Help From The Beyond

John thought the dimly lit séance room was spectacular, a mix of the macabre peppered with Victorian furnishings. A stuffed deer head loomed out from one wall, its glass eyes watching every move. In a darkened corner was a coffin set upright with a viewing window in its lid.

An attractive looking stone fireplace somehow became alive with clutching white gloved hands that acted as mantles, while a framed butterfly collection hung ominously nearby, making one feel that he or she just might be the next addition.

A large, six shaded chandelier with a centered, half globed light shown down upon a thick oval table with a Ouija board and a deck of Tarot cards. The ceiling was a canopy of dull white, almost pleated fabric that resembled the look of material one would expect to see inside an expensive coffin. Black and white 19th century photographs of sad, stone faced women in mourning clothes dotted the walls.

But by far the most impressive piece of décor was the ominous Angel of Death painted above the fireplace. It appeared to rise up towards the ceiling, its wings spread wide in an effort to capture lost souls, while its skeleton-like face smiled in perverse satisfaction. John wondered to himself if that is what his tormentor Death truly looked like behind the various costumes of humanity he presented from time to time.

The participants seated themselves around the table. Pat lowered the thermostat while Jen lit a few candles and some incense sticks to help set the mood. She then sat down on the almost throne like oak chair at one end of the oval. John sat to her right, followed around by the senior couple and the uneasy family of four.

Pat lit a final incense candle on top of the coffin, then turned the chandelier's dimmer switch to low, closing the creaking door slowly behind her. John wondered if that sound was deliberate, but it certainly did the trick, as the children stiffened in their chairs and gasped until the grating noise ceased.

Jen went about setting the ground rules and tone for the proceedings. "I want all of you to close your eyes and breathe deeply with your hands positioned palms down on the table. There's no need to hold hands. Try to cleanse your minds of any outside thoughts and fears. Continue to breathe slowly and rhythmically as you concentrate on clearing your minds. It's important to have a clean slate as we enter together into the great beyond."

One of the children became frightened. "Mommy, I don't think I can do this after all. Kyle, are you scared, too?"

"It's OK Jenny," the boy responded bravely to his sister. "We can do this together. Nothing will happen to you."

"That's right," Jen interjected. "I wouldn't let any little girl with the same name as me to be harmed in any way. Now let's stay quiet for a moment longer...There, that's better; the atmosphere is calm and peaceful. Now, who would like to go first? A volunteer is always preferable in starting these proceedings."

She looked over at John to her right and smiled slyly; "How about you stranger? Care to take a turn on the Ouija board before we move onto the tarot cards?"

John was amused. "What exactly do I have to do?"

"Just ask the spirits a question and see if anyone feels the need to answer you, but pick up the planchette, that's the pointer, while you're asking your question."

Tom broke into the conversation. "Yeah, ask the spirits if the Yankees have any takers for that freakin' bum A.J. Burnett." His wife Anne kicked him into silence with a vengeance.

John dutifully picked it up and began with a simple question, fully expecting nothing to occur. "Is there anyone here with us in this room who would like to contact me?"

With a bit of a tug, the planchette moved slowly from the center of the board, past the letters of the alphabet, and to the word YES in the top left hand corner. John had a look of disbelief on his face, but Jen was the only person who picked up on it. Everyone else thought it was a hoax. She quickly picked up a pen and sheet of paper.

"Ask it another question. I'll write down the reply as it's being spelled out."

John was becoming interested; "And what exactly is it you want to tell me?" His hand holding the planchette glided across the board toward the alphabet and then suddenly began jerking to letters in such rapid succession that he could not keep track of the words being formed, but Jen could. Finally, his hand stopped, and he looked at her.

"Did you get it all? What did it say? What is the message?"

She appeared puzzled as she read the words. "The message says: **JOHN- THEY KNOW- THEY ARE COMING.** Quick, find out who's reaching out to you!"

He cleared his throat before speaking, trying not to sound alarmed. "Who is here that is trying to help me?"

The planchette inched slowly over the alphabet, so slowly that John did not need Jen's help this time. The word spelled out was **DUMAINE**. His mouth dropped in awe as he stared at the board in silence for a moment, then looked around to his parlor mates, and finally, to Jen.

"Please excuse me. I have to go. Jen, I'm sure that I'll see you again…I..I hope."

She was trapped in the middle of the séance and so could not protest, but her face was etched with concern. Jen sensed that something was terribly wrong.

"All right; you can always find me at the Visitor's Center. Come see me if you need any help, or for that matter, just come see me."

John staggered out of the room and into the bookstore. He fully understood the message relayed to him. Pat was helping a customer with some book inquiries when she spied him out of the corner of her eye.

"Leaving so soon? Is everything all right?"

He never answered as he walked out of the bookstore onto the pathway leading to the sidewalk and the driving rain. It was coming down harder than before, but John had forgotten his umbrella in the séance room, not that it mattered. He had more important things to worry about now. He was being stalked, and to make matters worse, he was beginning to feel weak again from hunger.

People jostled him unapologetically on the busy sidewalk as they rushed to find shelter. It was then that he caught the scent of rotting meat coming from someone in the crowd. Yes, someone or something had picked up his trail.

What about that Dhampir? He cut across Baltimore Street to the rear of the public school buildings and took to the sky, lighting down on the rooftop of his blessed sanctuary, the north side of the Evergreen Cemetery Gatehouse.

His head was spinning with questions. How was his master Dumaine able to contact him, and how did he know that John was in danger? Ouija boards were supposed to be nothing more than parlor games for adults to spice up a dull evening. He never believed in them before, but this experience had changed his mind. He had to stop for a moment to try to reason this all out.

John decided that he needed to put himself in the mindset of his trackers. If they were attempting to locate the lair of a night creature from 1860's Gettysburg, just where would that creature find comfort and safety? The answer was an obvious one to him now; in the very Civil War era buildings that were still standing today, particularly one in a cemetery—-the Gatehouse. Evergreen was no longer a viable safe haven.

John took to the sky again as the rain began to let up slightly. He needed to feed and find shelter before dawn, or his victory celebration over the Ancients of the Vampire Council was going to be a short one. He set his course to the south as he flew over the darkened battlefield. All was quiet and still as he surveyed the landscape. Even the headlights from the vehicles of the park rangers were absent this evening.

The rain had changed the routine of many people. This would be the perfect time to locate a new haven and scour the area for an acceptable food source. Just then John detected movement along a road near the foot of East Cemetery Hill, so he decided to investigate. Perhaps it was some Freemasons he could ambush before they could report back to their lodge.

He set down in the branches of a nearby oak and watched in fascination. A man in a pickup truck was backing his rear fender up to the front of a granite monument and pushed the top portions of it over onto the grass. He got out quickly, bent over to inspect the base, and let out a string of expletives before hopping back into the truck to drive away. The rain was now tapering off to a thin drizzle.

So this is what the term vandalism meant, John thought to himself with disgust. Whatever the reason for this man's actions, they were not going to soothe John's rising anger. He set down lightly on the roof of the pickup truck's cab and waited a few moments as the driver attempted to make his way back into Gettysburg proper.

But that was not about to happen. In a flash John broke through the passenger window and grabbed the startled man by the throat as he spoke with his teeth clamped shut.

"Just keep this car moving and find a quiet spot where we can be...ALONE...Do you understand me?"

The bug eyed driver tried to shake his head up and down to signify a yes to the question, but John's hand was in the way, throttling him. He loosened his grip slightly as the pickup made its way along the Baltimore Pike away from the safety of town. The driver sensed that also, and he began to squirm and run his hands nervously along the steering wheel. John stared at him intently before speaking.

"Make a turn up ahead soon and stop this contraption so we can...talk things over."

The driver saw another car approaching from the opposite direction and thought for a moment about sideswiping it, but then changed his mind and made a right turn onto an even darker road before coming to a slow stop on the grassy shoulder. He took his hands off the wheel and placed them in the air in a sign of surrender. John released his grip but moved closer as he spoke.

"Who are you to desecrate that monument? Why would you do such a thing? It was placed on the battlefield to pay tribute to the honor and valor of soldiers long gone."

The man answered in a rush; "No need to get your shorts in a bunch, friend. The name's Jasper Fields and I'll tell you the whole truth, so help me God. My uncle did the same thing about 20 years ago to this very monument after he heard a rumor that there were some Civil War relics hidden in its base.

They were there all right, and he made a pretty penny on their sale. I just thought that maybe when they got around to puttin' the stone back up, someone would replace the items too, but there was nothin' this time, nothin'. You can't blame a man for tryin' now, can you?"

"You're right," John replied coldly. "I can't BLAME you, but I WILL KILL you." He grabbed him with both hands and squeezed his prey like a lemon. Jasper flailed about the cab in an attempt to get away, but John held him fast, until the man pulled a cigarette lighter from the dashboard and scorched the mad stranger on the arm, causing his temporary release.

Before John could resume his stranglehold, Fields blurted out a last gasp plea. "WAIT A MINUTE! I got some information that's worth my life. I SWEAR! Me and this other dude are supposed to blow up some niggers at the Visitor's Center a little more than a few hours from now. I just snuck away to take care of my personal business here at the monument first before we sealed the deal. I left him asleep in our motel room. You can still stop him if you hurry."

John was so shocked at this revelation that he turned his head slightly away from Jasper towards the direction of the Visitor's Center. He was fortunate enough to catch the glow of the cigarette lighter as it swung just wide of his left eye. Fields had missed his one chance, and John had had enough.

"You miserable bastard; I'm going to make a meal of you...just before I rip your head off."

That said, John lurched on top of the screaming man, ripped into his neck, and sucked deeply. He could feel his strength returning with each swallow of the warm, pulsing liquid. The squirming stopped in a moment, and John drank to his stone dead heart's content.

When Jasper was close to death, John stopped and looked into the face of his glaze-eyed captive with an evil grin.

"And now for the grand finale, you low life dog."

He shoved his hand up through the underside of the man's jaw and tore off the head in one quick jerk. The body quivered uncontrollably for several seconds before going limp and sliding down in the driver's seat towards the floorboard.

John unceremoniously scooped up the body parts of the unlamented Jasper Fields and took to the air for a third trip, although at low altitude on this occasion. He searched for a brief period and placed the head in a deep ditch and covered it with leaves, then hid the body in the crown of a large, leafed out sweet gum tree.

John recalled the Indian belief that the body's condition at the time of death was exactly how the person would return in the afterlife. If that belief held a grain of truth, then John surmised the late Mr. Fields would encounter a slight communications problem for all eternity. But Jasper was not the only one with a problem. John had to make a decision—find a safe haven before dawn to insure his existence, or save the lives of strangers.

To make matters worse, that decision was suddenly compounded by an unexpected obstacle. He began to feel lightheaded and nauseous, sensations he had not experienced since his incarceration way back in 1863 years ago.

John soon found himself being drawn like a magnet swiftly over the battlefield, passed Cemetery Ridge, the Peach Orchard, the Wheatfield, and to the summit of Little Round Top.

He had no physical control over his movements, and he had not the slightest idea why. John was headed for what could only be described as a magnificent castle, albeit on a small scale. It was constructed of rough-hewn, gray granite blocks that totaled in excess of 40 feet long, with a central arched through-way allowing pedestrians to access hidden spiral stairs leading to a castellated observation deck for an excellent view of the valley below.

John was being sucked directly into an adjoining round turret topped with a finely chiseled Maltese cross, almost as though he was a leaf floating on the water above a deadly vortex. He slammed unceremoniously into an interior wall face first, and then slipped into a restless unconsciousness before he could catch a glimpse of the unseen power that commanded him. However, he was able to make out the faint sounds of a short, chant-like incantation before the blackness surrounded him— **"Dormite, Hostes Mei, Ubi Statis!"**

CHAPTER 22

Sacrifice and Salvation

J ohn awoke a short time later with a splitting headache and blurred vision. The last time he felt this bad was after a long night out at Hagan's Tavern with his school chums from The Agricultural College of Pennsylvania in the fall of 1860. Unfortunately, he was not in his bed this time, but on the granite floor of a turret room atop a military monument, AND he smelled rotting meat.

He rubbed his temples and took a breath before attempting to orient himself. Although he succeeded, he was greatly disappointed. The first thing he saw was the policeman who gave him a ride to the Visitor's Center, Jack Ferguson. He was squatting behind a small orange flamed fire on the floor, his hands full of strange twigs and branches.

"Oh, I see that you have regained your senses; good. We were just about to begin the ceremony."

John rasped out a few questions. "What ceremony are you talking about? Where am I?"

"If you must know, you are inside the 12th and 44th New York Infantry Regiments Monument. It was designed by General Dan Butterfield, the first colonel of the 12th New York, and it was officially dedicated on July 3, 1893. There are a number of bronze tablets built into the walls that tell the reader about the regiments, muster rolls, etc. Well now, that about wraps it up, YOU FILTH! It's time to rid the world of another night creature."

"How...how did you know..."

"That you were a VAMPIRE? Very easily, I'm afraid. Remember our little joy ride on the Baltimore Pike the other night? I couldn't quite make you out in the rear view mirror while I was driving. At first I thought you were just in my blind spot, but after I dropped you off, I noticed the crack in the corner of the mirror...that's all it took, I'm afraid.

It was actually a great stroke of luck that I was driving by on patrol when I did. My colleagues and I have been trailing you ever since. Oh, say hello to Messrs. Harris and Nicoletti. They're first degree Freemasons of Good Samaritan Lodge #336. I myself am a third degree Mason, but you may have guessed that by now."

John peered into the shadows and saw two men standing on either side of their Master; both were sporting mimosa branches around their necks for protection, and each held vials of what John deduced was holy water. He wondered why they did not simply have stakes and mallets at the ready to finish him off with while he was unconscious. Ferguson deduced what John was thinking from his expression.

"I know, I know; why the drawn out procedure. This is actually safer for us. You see, you could have awakened while we were busy staking you out of existence; that could have put us in danger of being sliced and diced...or worse. You will notice that you can't move at the moment, the result of what I refer to affectionately as my rigor mortis incantation while you were taking your little nap before.

Once I finish the fire ceremony, a time tested ritual loosely copied from the Bulgarian Djadadjii vampire hunters, you will be shape shifted into the bottle held by Mr. Harris over there, and then Mr. Nicoletti will walk over and cork it shut. I will then cast the bottle into the fire and...POOF, one less vampire."

Ferguson began to delicately place leaves and branches into the fire, making sure to keep them in proper sequence. "We begin with ivy leaves...followed by hazel...larch...and willow twigs...and then complete the ceremony with elderberry branches. You're beginning to feel disoriented again, aren't you, filth?" The fire crackled and turned a scarlet red color.

John didn't want to dignify the Mason's question with what would have been an obvious yes, so he turned away and suffered in silence. It appeared that he had made a miraculous escape from the Devil's Den for naught, as Ferguson began the final incantation.

"Omne Flammans Flamma Purgatus, Domine Extinctionis Et Signum Regenerationis, In Mea Manu Ens Inimicum Edat! Flagrantia Rubicans!"

John felt his entire body start to dissolve and drawn reluctantly towards the bottle held by the smiling Harris. He once again put himself in the place of his enemy. The ritual was most probably designed to overcome an unwilling subject. But what would happen if the subject offered no resistance at all?

It was all John had to go on. He went limp and was instantly propelled towards Harris. This enabled John to be in close enough to him without having lost his physical form. The results were deadly. In one quick jolt, John smashed into Harris, throwing him against the wall in a sickening thud as he slid to the floor and dropped the bottle. There had not been enough time for the mimosa to ward off any evil intentions.

John then turned on Nicoletti, who had stiffened in fear and clutched desperately at his own mimosa necklace for his physical well-being. But John had other plans. He gazed into the Freemason's eyes and gave him a mental command, which was followed seamlessly. Nicoletti suddenly threw himself onto the still sitting Ferguson and strangled him with his bare hands.

211

There was nothing the startled and defenseless Master could do except flail and grunt until he passed out in a purple faced mask of death. His murderer stood up and looked to John for further instructions. Without another word, John cocked his head in the direction of the turret window slits, and the horrified Nicoletti ran to one and jumped screaming to the rocks below.

While John had overcome a most impressive set of obstacles, his unknown adversary back at the Super 8 Motel had important issues of his own to deal with.

"I don't have a fucking CLUE where he is, August. When I set the alarm last night for 4:00AM, I told him to try to keep his mind off the job ahead of us and get some sleep. He looked a little nervous, but I never thought the son of a bitch would punk out on me. He's AWOL, and his truck's missing, so I'm certain that he's gone for good. I'd better get the hell out of here before the SWAT team shows up."

"No…if Jasper had gone to the police, you would be calling me from prison right now. The most likely scenario is that he got cold feet and simply snuck out before you woke up. This is entirely my fault. I thought that he was up to the task, but it appears he can't be trusted after all. He betrayed my trust with cowardice.

After the dawn event, I want you to track Fields down and show him what we do to those who go weak in the knees…and make sure that you do it slowly. You don't think there'll be a problem without him to spot for you?"

"If I position my van in a certain location of the parking lot, I should still be able to maximize the damage, give or take a few onlookers. It'll be difficult, but not impossible."

"Good; I knew that I could count on you, Luther. Remember, the Priesthood is counting on a successful demonstration of what a few really dedicated Americans can do. After this, our numbers will surge all across the country, and for you my friend, the sky's the limit as to where you'll end up in our new hierarchy."

"I appreciate your confidence in me, August. I'm going to head over to the Visitor's Center shortly. The sunrise services are set for about 5:45AM, but I'll need to get there a little earlier than I had planned to make sure I get the right parking spot with Jasper out of the picture."

"Do whatever you have to do to get the job done and done right, Luther. Call me when you're safely on the road and I'll update you on the various news reports. I know that you'll want a blow by blow description. You'll have earned it. Goodbye."

As Luther Stokes drove out of the parking lot and down York Street to the center of town, he couldn't help feeling that he was going to have a great day. Not only was he going to kill scores of shines, including former General and Secretary of State Colin Powell, but he would be catapulted into the Priesthood's Legion of Honor.

Perhaps it was best that he did it all by himself; now he didn't have to share the glory with the half-witted Jasper Fields. It would only add to his prestige.

He made his way up Baltimore Street to the Pike and the Visitor's Center. The parking lot nearest the National Park Services information kiosk was almost a quarter full already, but he was still able to find the spot he needed to park. Descendants of Company F of the 29th strode proudly up the main pathway in their Civil War re-enactment uniforms along with their families towards the Lincoln statue.

Luther whispered to himself with a fair amount of amusement as he watched them. "You scum buckets won't look too fuckin' good once I make my phone call; just keep on strutting up to Father Abraham. He's going to set you free aaall over again."

He got out of the van and glanced at his watch as he walked up to the Visitor's Center to check out the area. The sun would be up in about half an hour. The night sky was starting to lighten up as he reached the statue and checked out the crowd that was forming. Colin Powell was at the podium doing a meet and greet while two men in crisp, dark blue suits stood nearby.

Their faces portrayed no emotion, but Luther thought they were probably pissed to the gills that they couldn't wear their sunglasses to look more ominous. After all, a Fed without sunglasses while on protection detail had to feel, well, positively naked!

He shot a glance over to the row of arborvitae along the building's wall. The grass had been cut, but that was the extent of the intrusion, just as he had hoped. The green propane tanks still nestled comfortably behind them, waiting patiently for the signal to unleash their exquisite hellfire and shrapnel.

While Luther Stokes headed back to his van for the scheduled blast off, John Larson was circling the town, torn between the natural instinct of self-preservation and a deliberate action of self-sacrifice in the most literal sense. He had not as yet found a temporary haven, and dawn was fast approaching.

Furthermore, Jasper's last second confession of impending mass murder kept gnawing at him until he realized why. Although strangers, the men and women who were going to die were descendants of the USCT, the United States Colored Troops.

Those determined Civil War soldiers, mostly ex-slaves with some free Negroes thrown in for good measure, had fought for their freedom first and foremost; but that also meant they were ready to die if that meant it would bring about the downfall of the Confederacy and thereby save the Union.

Patriotism, his "passion" and last vestige of humanity that meant more to him than any other past emotion, would not allow him to abandon those descendants despite the fact that the ceremony would start at dawn. Unfortunately, John's anger had gotten the better of him when he dispatched Jasper Fields before he could literally squeeze out more relevant details.

Although he knew the general place and time, he still would be at a distinct disadvantage. He could not identify the accomplice, nor could he even begin to fathom what new methods of destruction had been devised since his incarceration at the Devil's Den. He made the decision to help anyway.

In a few moments he was above the Visitor's Center and flying just over the tree tops around its rear section in an effort to detect any motion from the woods. He saw no movement whatsoever, but he could not help but notice brightness on the horizon. His window of opportunity to save both himself AND the families of Company F was closing rapidly. He had hoped for some devious stealth maneuver from the back of the building, but the area was deserted.

That could only mean a frontal assault of some kind. He veered back, setting down in the brushy growth along the main road and began to walk briskly with some latecomers through the parking lot leading to the Center's walkway. It was getting brighter, and the automatic photo cells perched atop the poles dotting the perimeter of the lot began to turn off the light fixtures one by one.

John finally reached the Lincoln statue and the happy crowd that was clapping loudly for keynote speaker Powell, who had stepped behind the podium after a brief introduction. One of the blue suited Feds nearby kept a watchful eye on the proceedings, while the other did a complete 360 and faced the building, as there were staffers inside who came in early to catch the proceedings from a somewhat different vantage point.

But no one bothered to check the innocent looking corner of the building with the harmless row of emerald green arborvitae. John thought about what Jasper Fields had told him; that they were going to blow the people up. The throng of about 100 was beginning to bunch up as Powell started the speech with a story from his youth in the South Bronx.

John needed to think like the bomber he was stalking the same way he put himself in the place of his Freemason pursuers earlier. He could see no signs of explosive devices anywhere in the area, and even if there had been, the Feds would have noticed them, shut down the proceedings immediately, and cordoned off the area. And how was the bomb going to be detonated?

As he whirled slowly around in bewilderment, John noticed one of the Feds talking on his cell phone. Over the past few days, he was very impressed as he watched people communicate to each other with this splendid device without wires. That's when it hit him—a cell phone would trigger the hidden explosion.

The sun began to rise above the treetops. John scanned the crowd, and no one save that Federal Agent was on a phone. Everyone else was enjoying the speech with rapt attention. He put himself in his adversary's place one last time.

The as yet unseen bomber would need to watch the group at a safe distance at just the proper time in order to ignite his charges, regardless of their location; that meant he was either in the Visitor's Center or…the main parking lot!

John opted for the lot; it would be easier for the murderer to make a quick exit in an automobile, and provide an extra layer of anonymity with the extra distance. He bolted down the path, past the Park Service information kiosk to the lot, and there sitting in the driver's seat of his van with a cell phone in his hand was Luther Stokes. Their eyes met for just a moment, but in that moment John knew it was his man.

He flew on a line straight to the van and pulled the cursing Stokes out through the window. John's body temperature was beginning to rise now as they grappled on the blacktop for the cell phone. He felt the skin on his face beginning to burn and blister.

Luther was able to flip open the phone cover and dial three or four numbers, but before he could finish, John ripped the arm of the Phineas Priest out of its socket, then picked it up and rammed it down the throat of the screaming man.

John fell on his back in agony and watched a beautiful sunrise as it burned his eyes, his first dawn in 150 years. He slowly turned over onto his stomach and made a feeble motion towards Luther Stokes' van, but it was too late; his clothes were now starting to smoke, and his hair ignited.

He crawled ahead a few inches and then stopped short in front of a pair of black wing tipped shoes. John made a supreme effort and looked up. It was Death, resplendent in a gray, pinstripe suit. The figure smiled kindly and bent down.

"John, take my hand. It's time."

"Wh…where are we going?"

"Why, through the door to the next dimension, of course! Remember, I told you once before that I am ALWAYS there for those DESERVING of my help."

"What…what's it…like?"

"WONDROUS! Beyond your wildest dreams!

Author's Notes

Elizabeth Thorn was the wife of Evergreen's first Caretaker, Peter Thorn, who was away serving with the Pennsylvania 138th Infantry when Lee attacked Gettysburg on July 1, 1863. Despite the fact that she was six months pregnant, 30 year old Elizabeth and her family quickly buried over 100 Union soldiers under poor sanitary conditions after the fighting ceased.

She would eventually give birth to a daughter named Rose, but the child was sickly and eventually died in her early teens. Some say this was due to her mother's stressed physical condition during the difficult surroundings of her pregnancy period.

Both Peter and Elizabeth stayed on and cared for their beloved cemetery until 1875. The two passed away in 1907 and are rightfully buried in Evergreen. They sure don't make them like Elizabeth Thorn anymore.

All Persons Using Firearms In These Grounds Will Be Prosecuted With The Utmost Rigor Of The Law. This is a semi famous sign that may or may not have been in Evergreen Cemetery at the time of the battle. Some people are convinced that it was, while others say it is just one of the many tall stories that are part of the town's rich history. Since no actual photos or proof of the sign have ever been produced, I thought I'd have some fun and have John be the reason for the controversy.

Incidentally, in reference to the flat headstones, Union soldiers in the cemetery placed them on the ground whenever possible during the bombardments to avoid certain injury from the incoming artillery shells that could shatter them to pieces.

Political Conflict was a way of life in Gettysburg, and the Civil War only intensified the rift between Democrats and Republicans. The townsfolk banded together during the battle, but once it was over and the threat of Robert E. Lee was removed, old habits and feuds were renewed with a fierce vengeance.

A great deal of distasteful finger pointing occurred, and some took the whispers and innuendos to the next level by reporting their personal and political enemies to the town's Provost Marshall, bringing about a number of arrests.

The actual Charles Will scene depicted in the story is fictional, but his arrest and detainment was very real. Quite a few residents who harbored or fed Confederates were forced to prove their innocence to the charge of aiding and abetting the enemy in time of war.

ON the level...Widow's son...On the square...Mother...So mote it be. These are all Masonic words and phrases that hold significant meaning within the Order. I had originally planned on explaining each of the above, but I thought it would be better to let the left wing conspiracy theorists find out for themselves while they take a break from their investigations of the faked NASA lunar landing of 1969.

By the way, the secret **handshake** depicted between Freemasons Fuerst and Shannon is real, and there are actually a number of variations based upon one's standing within the Order. I strongly suggest that everybody watch closely how prominent international politicians and business leaders press the flesh from now on. The Illuminati rule the world!! Muuuah haha!!

Mumiani is an East African name for, you guessed it, vampire. As if the native inhabitants didn't have enough trouble attempting to stay clear of jungle beasts, drought, famine, poisonous insects, and disease, along came the mumiani. It's a wonder the continent is so overpopulated. Since slaves sold to farmers of the United States came from Africa, I decided to sprinkle in a bit of their folklore...or could it be their reality?

Captain Charles Roberts of the 17th Maine Infantry was the convalescent officer depicted in the Garlach house on Baltimore Street. Scores of wounded soldiers like Captain Roberts were cared for in private homes throughout the town for a number of weeks after the battle, many of them officers.

The elaborate story told by Captain Roberts to Catherine and Henry Garlach pursuant to his serious wounding in the Wheatfield is actually his near verbatim description that was taken directly from the Maine War Papers, (Volume I).

Henry Kyd Douglas was the youngest member of Stonewall Jackson's staff during Old Jack's heyday in the Shenandoah Valley. The story about the general getting caught in the fruit tree is in Douglas' personal memoir, I Rode With Stonewall, which is highly informative though dry reading. Wounded at Gettysburg, he was left behind but was eventually allowed to meander around the town for some 1860's night life while his wound healed.

A number of other captured Confederates, usually officers, were also able to accomplish this feat, much to the extreme embarrassment of red-faced Federal officials, who were eventually able to put a stop to the lax enforcement of confinement rules towards the grey clad prisoners of war.

Thomas Holmes is regarded as the Grand Kahuna of funeral embalming. His techniques with various preservative fluids, brought to prominence by his personal preparation of Colonel Elmer Ellsworth's body, gave thousands of deceased soldiers' family members solace when their loved ones' remains arrived home in good condition for a final farewell and burial.

He also made a good buck for himself in the process, as evidenced by his blatant, sliding fee scale. Now there I go again, deliberately ruining another feel good story.

Dhampir—This was a word used primarily in the Baltic region of Eastern Europe. It was meant to describe the offspring that results from the union of a human and a vampire. Of course, it's pretty hard to understand how something that's already dead, the vampire, could help produce a living being, but why cloud the issue with such trivialities?

The most famous Dhampir is, of course, actor Wesley Snipes, who made a ton of money with a string of successful "Blade" movies, only to be later convicted and given a three year jail sentence at a federal correctional facility for trying to hide his profits from the Internal Revenue Service. Such a silly Dhampir!

The traditional Dhampir of the Balkans was a hideous being with some form of physical abnormality that was meant to partially act as a tip off that this person wasn't quite like the rest of us. Also, mixing live and dead genes pretty much ensures that you won't have much of a future as a runway model.

I couldn't quite decide how to make my particular Dhampir appear grotesque, but then I remembered the 1961 William Castle movie "Mr. Sardonicus." It was about a man whose face was frozen solid in a wide, hideous grin.

This is a great, black and white horror movie that's worth checking out. The more you glimpse the character of Mr. Sardonicus, the more repulsive he becomes, but much like Cosmo Kramer, you just can't look away.

Hanover Junction was a major transportation intersection and telegraph station during the Civil War, and it was situated about 30 miles from the outskirts of Gettysburg. Prior to the battle, the railroad station was overrun by Confederates and suffered damage at the hands of the 35th Virginia Cavalry Battalion, also known as Lt. Col. Elijah White's Comanches.

GettysburgDaily.com was a great resource for background information on this subject, plus it has GREAT "then and now" photos, which I'm a sucker for.

What Hath God Wrought—This parting, hand written note left by the fictional Colonel Nagle at the Hanover Junction telegraph office was actually the very first message to be transmitted over the telegraph by its inventor, Samuel Morse. It fit nicely into the story at the time, so I slipped it in.

The Vampire Council—I came up with the physical description for the ancient vampires from the 1982 swords, sandals, and sorcery movie "The Beast Master," where full grown man-like bat creatures enveloped human prey in their wings and then proceeded to suck them dry, leaving only bones.

It was essentially a cheesy B movie about a young prince who could communicate telepathically with animals, sort of an early precursor to Dr. Doolittle. Most male moviegoers will only remember the delectable Tanya Roberts in skimpy animal skin clothing, but me, I just LOVED those creatures.

The Triangular Field is quite an interesting place. Located above the Devil's Den, it was the scene of hard fighting on Day 2, with the Confederates temporarily obtaining the upper hand. Today, it is one of the chief locations on the battlefield for reported ghostly sights and sounds. Furthermore, cameras of all makes and models have a habit of malfunctioning with great frequency there.

With that in mind, II thought it would be the perfect location for John to be tried by the Vampire Council, inferring to any Gettysburg buffs that this was the origin for the abnormalities of today.

The True Builders Of The Pyramids…The Meaning Of The Lines At Nasca… The Hidden Message Of Stonehenge… The River That Hides Mokele-Mbembe…The Way Through The Puerta de Hayu Marca… The Burial Site Of Alexander The Great… The Location Of Atlantis—-All of these strange, mysterious locations and subjects have tantalized scholars, historians, scientists, and sci-fi fans for centuries, so naturally I thought the ancients from the Vampire Council should have knowledge of them.

Unfortunately, they never actually give John the ANSWERS, which would have been the decent thing to do, since he was about to be imprisoned for all eternity. So, if your interest is piqued and you're curious to find out the possible explanations to the above enigmas...you'll have to do some research and look them up for yourself.

The Devil's Den Snake—One of the many interesting stories about the origin of the name for this famous rock formation near Little Round Top is the legend that a giant snake once lived under the rocks and would venture out occasionally and terrify the local farmers of Gettysburg.

Since John was going to be buried there, I thought I'd have the Vampire Council make reference to the snake. It was essentially a freebie, and too good to pass up, but I never did get around to John having any contact with the reptile. Maybe it's still down there somewhere, just waiting to be awakened by some screaming Cub Scouts, and then.....

Ginoosteeg Monteeju and **Noinjimo** were actually nonsense words made up by my twins Kyle and Jenny when they were about 4 or 5 years old. The words always sounded cool and somewhat alchemistic to me, so I wrote them down for future use and decided to recycle them when the Vampire Council tried and sentenced John. I also didn't want to use too much Latin, as JK Rowling has corned that market with her Harry Potter spells and incantations.

Speaking of Latin phrases, I was pretty much forced to give a few lines to the Master Freemason Ferguson towards the end of the story. Real Freemasons love Latin like Southerners love Moon Pies, so without further ado:

Dormite, Hostes Mei, Ubi Statis. This means: Sleep, my enemies, where you stand.

Omne Flammans Flamma Purgatus, Domine Extinctionis Et Signum Regenerationis, In Mea Manu Ens Inimicum Edat!

223

Flagrantia Rubicans! This means: Ever burning fire of purification, Lord of destruction and sign of rebirth, spring forth from my hand and throttle my enemy! Red blaze!

Tree & Brush Site View Clearing at selected locations within Gettysburg National Military Park, including the Devil's Den, has been ongoing for several years now. The purpose is to restore targeted areas to their 1863 appearance so that visitors can better visualize and understand what went on and why during the complicated, three day battle.

This was an innovative yet controversial idea, causing a great deal of angst within the environut community, but then again, what doesn't? I thought the tree and accompanying root removals would provide the perfect instrument for John's glass prison to reach the surface for his eventual escape.

The Phineas Priesthood is a white supremacy group that has some roots in Pennsylvania, so I thought it would be a smooth tie in with the story. The Priesthood has no true command structure per se, but there are some notable members, such as August Kreis.

This weirdo was (surprise) on the Jerry Springer Show, along with his darling family, and spewed forth some truly disgusting views that shall go unrecorded here. If you insist on checking it out, I believe you can still catch it on You Tube. The Priesthood does have a rudimentary tattoo of its own; it's described briefly in chapter 19.

Company F 29th Infantry USCT was a colored regiment within the Army of the Potomac that was formed in 1864. Although it got a late start, the regiment fought in a number of important campaigns— the Crater, Petersburg, Richmond, and Appomattox. In 2003, a re-enactment group was formed and adopted the same name. They have a great website—www.29thusct.com.

The Eternal Light Peace Memorial, The Pennsylvania Monument, and the 12th & 44th New York Infantry Regiment Memorial are three of my favorite monuments on the battlefield, so I was happy that I was able to incorporate them into the story. They are definitely worth checking out if you love architecture, and even if you don't.

The 153rd Pennsylvania Infantry Regiment Monument on Wainwright Avenue near Cemetery Hill is a modest granite piece that has been knocked over on several occasions. There is ongoing speculation on why this particular nondescript monument has been the target of vandals. The Gettysburg Daily previously posted a theory that someone keeps looking for artifacts rumored hidden inside the granite base.

Dr. Jamie Oradell, the veterinarian and would be comic depicted in the Pub and Restaurant, was modeled after my very own favorite nephew, Dr. Jamie DeSantis, a veterinarian at the Oradell Animal Hospital in Oradell, New Jersey. (It is whispered that neutering is his favorite pastime). He also does standup comedy at various clubs throughout the tri-state area. Go figure.

The Italian Obituary read by the aforementioned Dr. Jamie in his act was actually a copy of a typed joke found some time ago in my late father-in-laws personal effects. I merely spruced it up a bit in an effort to bring it up to date. I have no idea how old it is, or who penned it for that matter.

Since I can never remember my father-in-law actually telling a joke in the 15 years that I knew him, I suspect he really liked this one. I trust you did too; thanks Doug. (I can only hope that the Italian Defamation League doesn't get wind of this and kneecap me).

Ouija Boards have had quite a checkered history. Some people claim that they are nothing more than harmless parlor games meant to spice up a dull evening, while others swear that they are mystical portals to another dimension that have the capacity to release vengeful spirits and demons.

Personally, I tend to err on the side of caution and do whatever I can to steer clear of them, although I have done a sitting with a medium and also underwent a past life regression session. However, if you prefer to walk on the wild side, Parker Brothers, the famous game company, still sells them, including a glow in the dark Ouija board for that added touch of mystery. (I assume it costs more, too).

Death—My initial persona for the important character of Death, as portrayed in my first book, came from filmmaker Ingmar Bergman's iconic movie "The Seventh Seal," that is, a cold, dispassionate being better off left alone if you know what's good for you.

However, for the sequel I changed my mind and decided to make him a more likeable and even helpful character, albeit openly jaded and cynical, while still maintaining that air of mystery. I thought that this would make him more interesting to the reader, and it certainly was more fun incorporating him into the story, and provided sporadic periods of humor. FYI, the persona for Death in this story was based upon…yours truly.

Gail Borden is considered the father of condensed milk, securing a patent for its production in 1856. In 1864, he opened his first factory in the village of Brewster, NY, (my home), where Routes 6 and 22 meet. A two lane span over a wide stream at the intersection on Route 6 is named The Borden Bridge in his honor.

Condensing milk essentially meant removing much of its water content, preventing spoilage and vastly extending its shelf life. Tons of the popular liquid was shipped by rail to grateful Union soldiers for the remainder of the war. Confederates, on the other hand, were not so lucky, as their attention was fixed more on arms and munitions than creature comforts.

The factory continued to prosper for several generations, but with man-made changes to the surrounding geography, it was eventually forced to close in the mid 1920's. But don't cry; the Borden brand is still on grocery shelves, complete with its Elsie the Cow logo, and the recipe remains pretty much the same to this day. Now you know all about the history of condensed milk, which can come in very handy at parties when trying to impress the ladies.

David Wills was a practicing attorney in the town of Gettysburg during the time of the battle. He was also a driving force in the subsequent establishment of the National Cemetery there. His house, where John hid temporarily on the southeast corner of the "diamond," was also the place where Lincoln later stayed and polished up the final draft of The Gettysburg Address. The Wills House is now a National Park Service museum open to the public.

Chloroform was the anesthesia of choice for surgeons during the Civil War, the other alternative being ether. It was quicker to render the patient unconscious, and unlike ether, it was nonflammable—always a good thing around a battlefield.

The trick to this anesthesia was to find that perfect balance of chloroform and air for proper respiration. Too much of the liquid could be fatal, while too little meant that the patient was conscious during the operation—never a good thing.

Despite the regurgitated graphic movie depictions of screaming soldiers biting on wooden sticks or bullets while being cut into pieces by frazzled surgeons, (a segment from the John Wayne movie "The Horse Soldiers" immediately comes to mind), anesthesia was more readily available than previously thought.

Burial Detail on a Civil War battlefield was a grim and thankless task to be avoided if at all possible, and at Gettysburg it was no different. There was precious little pomp, and absolutely no circumstance. The purpose was to get rotting and bloated corpses below ground as quickly as possible.

Shallow graves only a few feet deep were hastily dug out of a combination of expedience and hope for a re-burial at some later date. If the deceased was lucky (a strange play on words, to be sure), he got a pine board with his name and unit scratched over the grave for easy identification. If the deceased was not so lucky, he remained where he was, unknown and forgotten except for those who knew and loved him in life.

The Cyclorama Painting exhibit and lecture mentioned in Chapter 17 does in fact takes place daily in the Gettysburg National Military Park Visitors Center. The painting, the brain-child of French artist Paul Philippoteaux, was one of four created by him in the 1880's, and depicts a spectacular panoramic scene of Pickett's Charge on July 3, 1863.

The painting is on the second floor of the museum. It is 27 feet high and almost 360 feet in circumference. A visit to Gettysburg would truly be incomplete without a viewing of this magnificent work. Of course, as I previously mentioned, it's at the Visitors Center, so you'll have to pay to see it.

Good Samaritan Lodge #336, located at downtown Gettysburg in the square, is a relatively nondescript masonic temple that was built in 1895. Meetings are held on the second Tuesday of the month. I have never ventured inside the building to check things out, so I don't know what they do there.

However, I can't help but think of poor Janet Leigh being chased around a lodge hall by a slew of middle aged men wearing tasseled red fezzes in the movie version of "Bye Bye Birdie."

The Fictional Investigative Freemason Fuerst from Chapter 4 is, in reality, my boss, Deputy Commissioner John Fuerst of the White Plains, NY Department of Parking. He replaced my previous boss, John Larson, who moved up a notch and is now the Commissioner of Parking. (Go John)! In case you haven't guessed by now, I'm a shameless, unabashed suck up, but it works.

N.B.—No trees were cut down or severely pruned during the writing of this story.

Bibliography

Nonfiction/Papers Reference Sources

The Civil War News, (July, 2008) Beyond the Gatehouse-Gettysburg's Evergreen Cemetery, by Brian Kennell, (2000)

Days of Uncertainty and Dread, by Gerald Bennett, (1997)

Divided by Conflict, United by Compassion, by Terry Reimer, (2004)

The Encyclopedia of Civil War Medicine, BY Glenna T. Schroeder-Lein, (2008)

Gangrene and Glory, by Frank Freemon, (2008)

Human Interest Stories of the Three Days Battle of Gettysburg, by Herbert Grimm, Paul Roy, & George Rose, (1995)

I Rode With Stonewall, by Henry Kyd Douglas, (1940)

The Maine War Papers, Volume 1, (1898)

The New York Times Archive, (July 7, 1863)

One Continuous Fight, by Eric Wittenberg, David Petruzzi, & Michael Nugens, (2008)

Spirits of the Civil War, by Troy Taylor, (1999)

Speaking with Vampires: Rumors & History in Colonial Africa, by Louise White, (2008)

A Strange and Blighted Land, by Gregory Coco, (1995)

The Vampire Book: Encyclopedia of the Undead, by Gordon
 Melton, (1999)

A Vast Sea of Misery, by Gregory Coco, (1998)

Vigilantes of Christendom: The Story of the Phineas Priesthood,
 by Richard Kelly Hoskins, (1990)

Internet Reference Sources:

dcMemorials.com

Farnsworthhouseinn.com

Friendsofgettysburg.org

Gettysburgdaily.com (Dec3, 2008; May 19, 2009)

Museumoftalkingboards.com

NPS.gov

29thusct.com

Negima.Wikia.com

Movie Reference Sources

Beastmaster, (1982)

Conan the Barbarian, (1982)

Mr. Sardonicus, (1961)

Star Trek: This Side of Paradise, Episode 24 (1967)

CPSIA information can be obtained
at www.ICGtesting.com
Printed in the USA
FFOW01n1309200214
3727FF